MW01141902

8/15/22

BRUNCH
with the
JACKALS

BRUNCH
with the
JACKALS

DON McLELLAN

thistledown press

Thistledown Press Ltd.
410 2nd Avenue North
Saskatoon, Saskatchewan, S7K 2C3
www.thistledownpress.com

Library and Archives Canada Cataloguing in Publication
McLellan, Don, 1951-, author
Brunch with the jackals / Don McLellan.
Short stories.
Issued in print and electronic formats.
ISBN 978-1-77187-050-4 (pbk.).–ISBN 978-1-77187-068-9 (html).–
ISBN 978-1-77187-069-6 (pdf)
I. Title.
PS8625.L438B78 2015   C813'.6   C2015-900483-7
C2015-900484-5

Cover and book design by Jackie Forrie
Printed and bound in Canada

Thistledown Press gratefully acknowledges the financial assistance
of the Canada Council for the Arts, the Saskatchewan Arts Board,
and the Government of Canada through the Canada Book Fund for
its publishing program.

Acknowledgements

Early drafts of the following stories have been published in *Other Voices* ("The Invisible"); *Joyland* ("The Green Honda"); *The New Orphic Review* ("Rapture", "East Side Rules", "The Robin's Egg", "Alice Bird"); *Found Press* ("Angels Passing"); *The Dalhousie Review* ("Sweet & Sour", "Toy Soldiers"); and, *Broken Pencil* ("Mothas").

CONTENTS

The American novelists Joseph Heller and Kurt Vonnegut attended a fundraising event held in an art patron's swanky digs. Weary but dutiful veterans of such events, the old friends retreated at the first opportunity to a corner, where Vonnegut observed, "I'll bet our host makes more in a day than we've made in our entire careers." "You're probably right, Kurt," Heller said. "But I've got something he'll never have." "What's that, Joe?" Vonnegut asked. "Enough," Heller said. The characters in this collection are linked by the same concern: None of them feel they have enough.

Toy Soldiers

THE BODY OF THE REBEL DARCY CORRIGAN had been dumped outside the armoury, a signature of the new provost. *Keep it up,* it said, *you could be next.* The provost prances through the village surrounded by a security detail, medals swinging from his lapels like a mighty pair of breasts.

The rebel leadership decided to hold the memorial service in a derelict farmhouse on Cobble Hill. Its tenants had been run off or jailed, the sheds torched. An ideal location, it was thought, for a safe house.

In the days leading up to the service rebels trickled in from every direction. A few — McCabe and Joyce — were grandfathers, men of strong views and loyal hearts. But most, like the deceased, were schoolboys. In another time and another place they might have passed an evening such as this one practising knots for a Scouts badge or corresponding with pen pals. Darcy had never kissed a girl.

His mother, an empty shell of a thing, keens behind a veil. She is accompanied by an elderly priest who has huffed and puffed his way to the summit, the reason for their tardiness.

"There's broth, bread, and a swallow of ale," Riley, the rebel leader, tells each new arrival. "When you've had your fill, we'll begin."

But before the priest can light the candles, a lookout bursts into the room.

"Jesus bleeding Christ!" he hollers, before scampering out the rear. They'd heard dogs and marching boots, the trailing lookout elaborates. He, too, exits speedily.

"Follow them, lads!" Riley orders. "Rendezvous at McDonaugh's Bog."

Kevin tipped the tin box: toy soldiers tumbled like jacks across the linoleum floor. His ma was in the kitchen making meat pies. If he ate the greens and proved accurate with his numbers there'd be pudding afterwards. The smell of frying onions wafted along the hallway, ducking into the sitting room where he played most afternoons. Until his lungs improved, *if* they improved, one of the Brothers would drop off his lessons.

Each toy soldier was the height of a matchstick, and each struck a different pose: many charged, some fled, others kneeled. This one wielded a blade, that one levelled a rifle — *pk-k-ew! pk-k-ew!* Most were plastic, but a few — those from an earlier era — were made of metal from lead moulds or carved in softwood. They didn't make tin soldiers anymore.

Most of Kevin's warriors were cowboys and Indians, torsos pierced with arrows, tomahawks buried in limbs, the faces of settlers and savages contorted by victory or injury. He kept the Roman legionnaires and gladiators in an empty butter tub. They carried spears and truncheons, their pectorals taut, biceps bulging. The Second World War set, a Christmas present from his da, came with tanks and jeeps.

Individual pieces were sometimes inserted into a packet of crisps, a promotion of some sort, or advertised on a cereal box, one of a collection. For Kevin's last birthday Brother Mahoney had given him a secondhand set called Rebels on the Run. He'd spotted it at a flea market in McCarthur Road.

"There might be a few pieces missing," the Brother said, "but they don't make these anymore. The government forbids it."

"What government forbids play?" Kevin asked.

"Ours. They say it inflames the passions."

When he was setting up a scene, and when he didn't have enough soldiers to make an engagement seem real, Kevin conscripted pawns and bishops from the family chess set to serve as extras. He arranged brigades and divisions atop the mantel, which he fancied as high ground, positioning the combatants on the dresser (a forest), or in a flanking manoeuvre on the floor (the battlefield). By the time his da returned from work, the tea thermos clanking inside his lunch pail as he came up the alley, the room would be a cauldron of exploding missiles and flying shrapnel. Corpses would be everywhere.

Kevin invented dialogue and mimicked death throes, sprawling across the sofa, a fallen hero. These make-believe clashes could transport him to the far side of the world, to military campaigns centuries away from the damp, windowless room with its low ceiling and peeling wallpaper. When rockets were exploding, a cavalry charging, he was oblivious of the affliction ravaging his body.

One night his da brought home co-workers from the shipyard. They got into the drink; tobacco smoke filled the kitchen. Their shouting faces were soon bobbing like red apples around the table as they discussed first football, then the pony races, and finally the rebellion that years later still inflamed the passions. The commotion woke Ma, who got up and made a batch of chips. Kevin's da sang a loyalist ballad so lovely some of the men teared up.

Of those who bolted from the farmhouse, only seventeen rebels make it to McDonaugh's Bog. McCabe and Joyce are among the missing. The capture of a senior insurgent is celebrated by the military authorities, as oldtimers know who's who in the movement and where the explosives are hidden. Intelligence, they call it, a curious term, Riley always thought, for what is often preceded by the bashing in of a brain. Curious as well considering how much intel proved inaccurate.

The rebels have nine rifles and four revolvers, no match for the bunch pursuing them. Provisions amount to a single water can, nuts, apples, and some sausage. In calculating rations, the rebel leader remembers the boys are not of a generation accustomed to going without. For some, this would be the first night away from their beds.

Before joining the struggle Riley had taught school. It was the reason they had him working with the new recruits. He and Marion had lost John, their only child, a week after he'd graduated St. Helen's Collegiate. John had bristled with anger — not just about the occupation, but anger at the world, at what it wasn't and never would be. Very much like his father had at that age.

Marion disapproved of Riley's decision to avenge the death. It won't bring him back, she wailed. And how will we survive on such a meagre stipend? But she learned to accept his absences, or at least to hold her tongue, and she never asked what, exactly, he did on behalf of the cause. She took a job in a pastry shop.

Riley catches sight of the moon poking through the forest canopy. At this hour he supposes she'll be fresh from the bath, running a brush through her hair. The thought excites him still.

"Can we smoke?" At home such impudence would earn the boy a cuffing.

"It could be your last," Riley replies. He speaks softly to the recruits, as though he's teaching mathematics again. He'd not been so considerate with John. The rebel leader was different then, more demanding, as young fathers sometimes are with their own.

"When the enemy lights a fag, a sniper loads his weapon," he warns. "When the smoker reaches over to light a second cigarette, the shooter adjusts his scope.

The third man to share your match will get it between the eyes. His girl won't recognize what's left."

McGinnis, one of the new boys, asks, "What do we do now?" He's shivering. Or trembling.

Riley waves them closer.

"We can head for the mountains and divide ourselves into groups," he says. "If yours is followed, divide again; they can't get us all. Or we can take the ravine to the shore. Some of the fishermen are patriots."

"You don't sound very optimistic." McGinnis again.

"An optimist invented the airplane," Riley says. "A pessimist gave us the parachute."

Back on Cobble Hill, in the chaos of flight, most of the rebels hadn't time to collect overcoats and caps, a problem if they elect the higher altitudes. As for the shore, Riley wonders how many, including himself, have the stamina. The terrain is steep and uneven, treacherous in the dark. Any injured will be left for the provost.

Several of the boys can recite the poetry of the struggle, and they do so now, fleeing through the woods for their abbreviated, uneventful lives. Wars couldn't be waged without this hunger for glory and adventure. Young and dumb, McCabe liked to say of the recruits, and full of cum.

"Those are our options?" asks McGinnis. "The mountains or the sea?"

"We can pray," says Riley.

"For what?"

"For fog. A fog as thick as your mother's stew."

"Why fog?" queries another.

14

"Because a bullet can't find its mark," Riley tells them, "and it confuses the dogs."

The rocks tiling the floor of the ravine are slick with algae; progress is slow. An hour into the retreat and movement is heard in the bramble. Riley signals a pair of boys to investigate but, before they can, something sails over the ledge. The impact empties a shallow pool.

The boys lean in. Matches are sparked.

"It's Dempsey."

Riley remembers him. Son of a pig farmer. None too bright, but a grand marksman.

"I called for a rendezvous," Riley says. "You're a long way off."

"Aye, sir," Dempsey says. "But I don't know that word."

"Rendezvous?"

"I know pigs, sir. I didn't study the foreign languages."

Kevin threads a lace from his boot, stretching it into an arc on the linoleum — a half-moon shoreline. Exhausted, the rebels dig a shallow trench there. Behind them, waves gently slap the sand. Riley parleys with Allan, an older boy who's distinguished himself on several missions. In the absence of a McCabe or a Joyce he's promoted to second in command.

Allan says, "This trench will soon fill like a pothole in the rain. What then?"

Riley addresses the boys, "Who's the fastest runner?"

All-eye McGinnis.

"You should see him move a football."

Riley hands him a revolver.

"O'Brien's shack is beyond the dunes," he says. "He has a boat."

McGinnis swigs from the water can and takes a bite of sausage. They bid him safe passage, and off he goes.

Allan says to Riley, "Maybe they didn't pick up our tracks. I haven't heard the dogs."

In the sitting room Kevin rolls up one of his ma's magazines and lifts it to his lips.

Woof-woof!

Riley gobbles an apple and chucks the core. The proximity of the splash concerns him. The soldiers have dug a trench facing the redoubt, settling in for a siege. Their campfires flicker along the beach.

"We wouldn't be in this mess if more joined us," Allan says, a challenge of sorts.

"The struggle has been going on for a long time," Riley obliges. He enjoys a spirited joust, but preferably in the pub, and after a few. Not now. "But you're right, Allan, blindness has its advantages."

He walks the length of the trench. Several of the boys are praying. A few weep quietly, and from the stench he suspects one has soiled his trousers. He wonders how many will cross into manhood this night, and how long they'll live to enjoy it.

"They'll come at first light," he says. "Those with revolvers, shoot the dogs first. The rest of you fire selectively when I give the order — everybody but Dempsey. You take the sniper's rifle, son. Target the provost."

"I don't know what he looks like," Dempsey says.

"He'll be the one with all the medals, and the farthest from the fighting. Pop that pig and they might write a song about you."

The rebel leader had never been so forthright with the recruits. Why now? He hadn't been himself since the night they snatched a young lance corporal returning to his base. The boy was bold, probably from the drink, refusing to answer Riley's inquiries. It was a valiant choice: talk might have delayed the sentence, but talk wouldn't have commuted it.

Riley unholstered his weapon.

"Do it!" the corporal spat. "Fekking terrorist!"

Riley had asked John to stay home that night; he and Marion had a bad feeling. There were roadblocks all over the county. "I'm no coward," John had said. Brave words, a fool's words.

The lance corporal was no coward either. They'd rolled his body into the ditch and covered it with leaves.

Kevin flattens a sheet of newsprint and spoons more sand from his pail: the beach. He'd brought the stuff back from a holiday. He imagines a strip of blue fabric as the rising tide.

"Wash up, luv," his mother, poking her head into the sitting room, sings. "Your da will be home shortly."

Kevin studies the scene. Seawater seeps into the rebels' trench. Opposite, the soldiers prepare for the attack. Baying dogs tug at their tethers.

"I'm almost finished here, Ma."

The fog is drawn to land like metal to a magnet. McGinnis crosses the dunes, desolate and damp in the hours before daylight. He wonders if he has any hero in him, if it's like broad shoulders and a sharp eye, a quality handed out at birth. He skips across the barnacled rocks, a striker charging downfield. The roar of the crowd is deafening.

A blow sucks the air from him. Men close in as he flails on the ground. Someone plants a boot on his chest.

"Where might you be going?"

A panting hound sniffs his crotch.

The fog makes landfall at dawn. It separates the adversaries, a wall of ambiguity. When the sky pales, it lifts; the soldiers advance. But they are too late. The rebels have vanished. Brine swirls between the provost's boots.

The fishing boats fan out across the bay; Kevin's da arrives home. "Your food's getting cold," his mother calls. On the deck of a trawler the pig farmer's son takes aim. Kevin gazes down upon his creation. *Pk-k-ew!* he cries, and at the flick of a finger the provost topples into the sea.

Angels Passing

THE CREW HAD BEEN REPAIRING THE DIKE for weeks without respite, beginning each day before sunrise, stopping only when it became too dark to continue. But then the monsoons swept in from the southwest, washing out the road. The workers were given a much-needed hiatus.

The boss addressed the men as they jostled for their pay packets.

"Those whose names are on this list" — he hammered a leaf of rice paper to a banyan tree — "be back here when the rains stop. The others, return to your farms."

Choi's name was near the top of the list. The youngest of the labourers, he had not only enough energy remaining after the evening noodles to compete in the camp's wrestling contests, but the strength and agility to win them.

He had fallen in with a carefree youth named Soo, who suggested they wait out the downpours at an inn located in a neighbouring district.

"That's a long way to walk for a bed," Choi said.

"Have you never heard the song, 'The Inn of Tender Embraces'?" asked Soo. He whistled a few bars from the traditional melody. "Like the lyrics say, 'One night at the inn will change your life.'"

When the fighting stopped and a truce had been signed, the order instructed me to help facilitate reconstruction in the provinces. Trang was my driver and translator. His wife Woo-ling managed the order's affairs and cooked and cleaned. The couple lived in a cottage behind the rectory.

"Have I told you the story about the Inn of Tender Embraces, Brother Michael?" Trang asked me. "People say it's true."

I thought at the time that Trang shared such yarns to help pass the hours and to practise his English on our long, bumpy drives into the interior. A few were classic tales my assistant claimed as his own, confident I wouldn't recognize them. He also relayed bits of gossip from the market, random thoughts that popped into his head — anything, it seemed, to void the quiet as our jeep skimmed over the bomb-scarred landscape.

It was during one of Trang's long-winded accounts that I thought of Brother Roderick. As part of our preparation for a life of sacrifice, seminarians are required to endure a year of silence. Brother Roderick counselled the novices.

"Occasionally a lull will occur between two people," I remember him telling us. "Between friends, between man and wife, between strangers who may have struck up a conversation."

His Irish lilt is as soothing to me in recall as it was decades ago.

"You mustn't let the absence of words upset you," he continued. "Silence is an invitation to listen. It's not a pothole. There's no urgency to fill it."

"And why," asked one of the novices, speaking for many of us, "wouldn't we offer a word to move things along?"

"When it's quiet," replied Brother Roderick, "the angels are passing."

They arrived at the inn just as the gates were being secured for the night. The innkeeper considered their worth, then offered quarters above the stable.

"This will cost all of our savings," Choi said. "Maybe we should look for something less expensive."

"It'll be money well spent," Soo said. "Besides, it'll be dark soon and the nearest shelter is a long way off. The leopards feed at night."

And so the inn it was.

They were encouraged to bathe in a shallow pool upstream. Women the age of grandmothers washed the young men's hair and scraped the dead skin from their backs with coarse-bristled brushes. The woman assigned to Choi soaped his brawny chest, boldly allowing one hand to explore between his legs.

"They didn't make them like this when I was young," she said, giving him a squeeze. (Or perhaps Trang was embellishing again, concerned my interest was waning.)

Their clothing was whisked away to be laundered. For the duration of their stay the pair wore traditional silk robes emblazoned with the inn's signature. Identical attire rendered the guests equal in status.

After dinner they were invited to visit a beverage room.

"It was," Trang explained, "a kind of gentlemen's club."

"They played cards, did they?"

"Not exactly, Brother Michael."

"I understand, Mr. Trang. Please continue."

Unfamiliar with the power of bottled spirits, Choi quickly became inebriated. Although the girl in his lap was a beauty, full-bodied and eager to satisfy, as the evening unfolded he found himself drawn to an attendant, a timorous thing whose task it was to distribute a salty snack.

"A lovely to be sure," Soo agreed. "But if she isn't offered to customers, there must be a flaw."

"A flaw?"

Choi studied her figure.

"I don't see any — " But then his eyes settled on the imperfection. The girl was lame.

"She walked sideways, like a crab," Trang said. He consulted his dictionary. "She scuttled."

Polio, I assumed.

In the morning, the rain unabated and Soo sleeping off his over-indulgence, Choi climbed alone to the bathing pool. The same old woman scrubbed the young man's back. Again, she gave him a playful tug.

"Some of the guests enter by the back door," she cackled, exposing gums stained crimson by an herbal intoxicant. "Which are you?"

Later that morning Choi noticed the lame girl hanging the wash.

"I saw you last night," he said. He told her his name.

"Akia," she said.

"We'll be there soon, Brother Michael." The jeep strained to reach the summit of a forested hill. Trang shouted above the keening engine, "It's been closed for years!"

We coasted moments later into a clearing, stopping alongside the remains of a two-storey building. Tiles were missing from the roof, doors from their frames. Hardly what I had expected of the fabled Inn of Tender Embraces.

The unkempt gardens and crumbling masonry reminded me of a Latin term: *genius loci*. It means the ambiance of a place, what some of our young people these days refer to as a "vibe." The damage done to the inn reminded me of what discord and rancour could do to a country. Decay hovered over the place like a revolting smell.

"Musicians came from all over the country to perform here," Trang said. "Dignitaries would catch the train from the city. Foreigners, too."

Trang selected a room with a fine view of the valley, chasing off nesting doves with a clap of his hands. Half the ceiling was extant and half was open to the stars, so he threaded a tarp through the beams — a precaution, he said, against the sudden and heavy rains referenced in the song.

We gathered scraps of wood and built a fire in a bed of stones.

"This was the most expensive accommodation, Brother Michael. Only VIPs stayed here."

"Then we're in the right room, are we not, Mr. Trang?"

Woo-ling had prepared food for our journey. Each day's meal was wrapped in an elaborately embroidered fabric bound with a ribbon. As we worked our way through that evening's designated offering, it occurred to me that my assistant never spoke of his wife or their life together. Did they have children? I had no idea.

I always assumed this reluctance to share something of his private self was due to cultural dictate. But the longer I lived in the country the more I doubted it. I had never asked his age and he had never volunteered one, although other nationals freely revealed their years. He appeared to be at least a decade my senior.

Trang's explanation as to how he came to speak English — that he had a knack for languages — was also wanting. His fluency hinted at an education unavailable to most, the coaching of a native speaker perhaps, or a stint in the West. Had this been the case, why wouldn't he have said so?

Brother Winston, my predecessor, had clarified why all household business was conducted through Trang, never Woo-ling. It wasn't that she couldn't speak English; I had overheard her speaking it, albeit haltingly, to a

UN nurse. My colleague explained that it was viewed as improper in this part of the world for a woman to be seen in a lengthy conversation with a man not a husband or family member.

"Don't take it personally," Brother Winston said. "Their way of doing things has survived much longer than ours."

Woo-ling, then, by only entering my quarters when I was absent, was merely being a proper wife. I do know that many new converts were suspicious of a man like myself who had forsaken a wife for a belief. Their clerics made no such sacrifice.

I often caught glimpses of Woo-ling squatting in the garden, filling a basket with greens. Or leaning out the window of the cottage kitchen, tossing scraps to the birds. She seemed happy enough.

Rocking in our hammocks that first night at the inn, a welcome breeze from the valley tousling the leaves on the trees, Trang turned to me and said, "That's the moral of this story, Brother Michael."

He was referring, I realized, not to himself and Woo-ling, where my thoughts had been, but to Choi and Akia.

"When two people are truly in love, they don't have to say anything. It's . . . "

"Unnecessary?" I offered. "Ordained?"

"Yes, thank you, Brother Michael. Goodnight."

Choi and Soo were descending the stairs leading to the club when the manager, Mr. Lee, stopped them on the landing.

"Would you join me for a drink?"

Assuming an inquiry about their tab, perhaps a request for collateral, the pair followed him into a dimly lit room lined with private booths. They accepted the rice wine proffered but declined a turn at the opium pipe. An older Western man sitting alone in one of the booths studied the newcomers intently.

"I hope you're both having a good time," said Mr. Lee. "And so you should — you're both young!" He seemed particularly interested in Choi.

"I saw you at the bathing pool earlier. You're very strong."

"You should see him wrestle," Soo said. "Say, I don't see any girls in here."

"The girls are on the other side."

When Mr. Lee was called away on a staffing matter, the Western man motioned them to his table.

"This isn't for us," Soo said.

Mr. Lee reappeared before they could leave. He whispered into Choi's ear, "You could make a lot of money in a place like this."

We had been travelling for hours. While I poured over the maps, Trang nudged the jeep through the hordes straggling back to their villages: militiamen, the wounded, children unclaimed, women bloodied from indignities. They were drifting across the muddy fields as though in a trance, pleading for food, money, medicine. Trang advised against stopping. In my years with the order I had ministered in several countries divided by conflict, but I had never witnessed anything on this scale. With each successive war, it seemed, the more efficacious was the weaponry, the more successful the devastation.

Just as darkness settled in, our jeep blew a tire. Trang pulled over and reached for the spare. I noticed a group of children sitting by the roadside. I thought little of it, as children would often walk from their villages, most of which were still without power, to study their lessons under the lights lining the new highway.

This was not the case with these youngsters. As I was searching our trunks for the chocolate we carried for such occasions, Trang tapped me on the shoulder.

"Look, Brother Michael . . . "

A dog had been killed by a passing vehicle. The children were greedily devouring its entrails. We had interrupted their dinner.

After meeting with the village elders we raced back to the inn, washing down Woo-ling's meal with warm beer purchased at a field hospital. It was after midnight by the time we tumbled exhausted into our hammocks.

As I was drifting off Trang began whistling the melody, "The Inn of Tender Embraces," notification that it was time for another instalment of his story.

"Choi knew his parents would never accept a girl with a bad foot," he said, "a girl who worked in a place such as this. They would ask him, 'If her own family gave her up, why would we take her in?'"

"You didn't mention," I said, "that Akia had been given away."

"In those days, Brother Michael, if a family couldn't pay a debt, if there had been a poor yield, one of the children would be sold into bondage. Families were reluctant to give up a boy. Some girls worked in the kitchens of rich men and some were sold to brothels. If a family had a daughter who scuttled, well, the decision as to which child to sacrifice was an easy one."

"And the family," I inquired. "Would they never see their child again?"

"If the family came into some money, the obligation could be purchased. Anyone could take it over. But in this part of the world, if you're born poor, you die poor. It's only otherwise in fairy tales, or perhaps in great countries like yours."

For a moment the night belonged to the bullfrogs and the cicadas and the moonlight spilling through the pines, but between Trang and me, not a word. The angels were passing.

Finally he said, "Do our customs seem cruel to you, Brother Michael?"

"People everywhere can be cruel, Mr. Trang. No more in your country than in mine."

He never spoke again of the doomed young couple, and I never asked. Trang's tongue didn't stop wagging, however. Subsequently I heard about a boy who'd been separated from his mother only to be reunited years later; about a young man who successfully stowed away aboard a supply ship bound for America — heaven, to many, with its gleaming skyscrapers and well-stocked refrigerators.

That these stories invariably ended predictably did not disturb me. A happy ending was important to a population unfamiliar with one.

And then one day the telegraph arrived. My term of active service with the order had expired. A military convoy would transport me to the airport. Trang took the news hard. Though the order frowned on personal attachments, I assured him that in my retirement I would have ample time to write. We both knew I wouldn't.

He asked if I would join him for a farewell dinner. I had never been inside my assistant's residence, but I thought it might be formality to extend the invitation and formality to decline.. Even after two years in-country, the social customs of these lovely people remained Byzantine to me.

"But Brother Michael," he protested, "Woo-ling has prepared all your favourite dishes."

The feast, held the evening of my departure, must have cost Trang a month's wages. Many of the ingredients, not to mention the French cigarettes I loved, were only available on the black market, which could be an expensive, even dangerous undertaking. He presented me with a cigarette lighter, the kind you flip open with the thumb. I gave him all of my remaining American dollars.

Anyone familiar with my girth will not be surprised to learn that I did most of the noshing at this Last Supper, or that Trang, given what I've said of him, did most of the talking. Woo-ling remained in the kitchen — contentedly so, apparently; I could hear her singing above the clatter of pots and pans. She did deliver more food, but only during my visits to the privy behind the cottage, which, because of a sensitive bladder, were frequent. On my return to the table she would be back at the stove, the timing of her entrances and exits expertly choreographed.

When it came time to leave, both of us stifled a sob. I dashed outside once more, wanting to compose myself for the final farewell. On my return Woo-ling was stationed at her husband's side. With a nod from Trang she reached up and squeezed my arthritic neck. Though my knowledge of the dialect regrettably never surpassed rudimentary, I'm quite certain whatever she mumbled into my ear was heartfelt.

"Your car will arrive shortly," Trang reminded. "Allow me to see you to your door one last time."

On the path linking the two residences, he stopped.

"The lighter, Brother Michael — you've left it behind!"

As he flung open the door of the cottage I caught sight of Woo-ling, her arms piled high with dishes, scuttling across the floor.

I still have that cigarette lighter, although at my doctor's insistence I no longer have the habit that made it necessary. Even after all these years, particularly on nights a heavy rain lashes the window, I'll lose myself in its blue flame, and I sometimes catch myself humming the opening bars of that lovely song.

Invisible

JUST AFTER DUSK, A BANK OF FOG sifting into the channel, the captain of the freighter appeared on the bridge.

"Into the lifeboats!" he said. "Quick — while we still have this cover!"

On shore, before pushing off, one of the crewmen told the men and women left shivering on the beach, "We have to clear Customs. Someone will return for you in a smaller vessel. Stay out of sight."

Members of the panel looking into the deaths of undocumented workers mumbled, nodded, scribbled notes, sipped water. Translator Diane Ng dropped into her seat beside the detainee Ling Wa. The official leading the inquiry said, "What happened next?"

Ms. Ng addressed the four impassive mandarins. "They were cold and hungry. It was too wet for a fire. Some of the men went looking for shelter. They didn't realize it was an uninhabited island."

One of the panelists asked, "Are any of these men here today?"

"No," said translator Ng. "The body of one was discovered at the bottom of a cliff. The others were never found."

An eruption of whispers broke out in the public gallery; the follow-up question was inaudible. A few reporters slipped from the room. The senior panelist pounded the table.

"*Please . . .*"

To Ling Wa, the dark-suited quartet squinting over documents looked alike, grim and inscrutable. The widow Lao Shu murmured, "How do their mothers tell them apart?"

Guffaws rippled through their ranks, a welcome respite from the monotonous unreality of the proceedings. The four bureaucrats frowned identically, initiating another round of levity.

"If there are any more of these disruptions . . . "

Calm restored, a panelist spoke. The words gushed from the man's mouth like water through a gorge, their meaning intelligible to all but the dozen dazed souls being questioned. Even the translator could be opaque, as she spoke a dialect so unfamiliar that they often had to interpret her.

"They know," Diane said, huddling with the detainees, "that a few days later you were transported to a camp and put to work harvesting shellfish. They understand there was a full moon that evening."

"Take your time," the panelist said. "Start at the beginning."

The camp consisted of tents pitched around a trailer containing a generator, washrooms, showers, and a mess. It was run by a man known to them only as Andrew and his adult son Willy. The pair resembled each other in every way except the hair: the father's fell across his forehead like strands of kelp. Willy's was coarse as a shoe brush.

"I'm away, my boy's the boss," Andrew said. "Do as he tells ya. I'll hear about them that don't."

Father and son communicated with the harvesters by grunting and hand-waving. Sometimes their directives were understood, sometimes not. If necessary they would turn to Be Shing for help. Years of working for such operations had afforded the camp matron an abbreviated understanding of English.

"You peak Be Shing swo-wee, okay?" she advised Andrew. "Berry, berry swo-wee."

Willy used a mongrel canine to police dissent in the camp; at the tug of its leash Shep would bare its fangs. Andrew also warned the harvesters about the area's indigenous inhabitants.

"Chugs don't like nobody else diggin' here," he said. "Keep your distance, don't talk to 'em. A couple of years back cops found human remains in their cooking pots."

Ling Wa had noticed native children watching the harvesters, their dark eyes set in dark pie-shaped faces. They didn't seem angry or particularly hungry. She always waved to them; they always giggled and fled when she did.

"You have to double-check your totals," Lao Shu warned the others. Like Be Shing, the widow had picked up some English. "Willy doesn't cheat us like his father. He just can't count."

Lao Shu's linguistic abilities were a camp secret: their handlers spoke freely only around those they believed didn't understand. She informed Ling Wa of Willy's interest.

"Like that one?" Lao Shu had overheard Andrew ask as father and son sat by the campfire one evening. Ling Wa, spooning out the rice, was unaware her attributes were being evaluated.

Andrew drank from a bottle and passed it to his son.

"What you waiting for then, huh?"

Every day thereafter, Ling Wa sweeping out the tents, Willy would block her exit. The mutt stood guard. A fleshy palm smelling of fish smothered her protests.

"Wanna keep your job, little girl?"

When the elders learned of the assaults, the husky young harvester Kwok was assigned to shadow the girl. A rumour was circulated — tidings scripted for Willy's ears — that Kwok was an accomplished martial artist.

"It need not be true," said Lao Shu, author of the idea. "Only that The Idiot believes it so."

And it wasn't. Kwok was a quiet, mannerly boy sent abroad to pay down a family obligation. He wore his long hair slicked back like the pop stars he so adored, and he rarely removed his sunglasses, which to some Western eyes may have lent him a menacing countenance. Back home he'd chaperoned a sister.

"Just scowl occasionally," instructed Lao Shu. "Be Shing will give you an extra scoop of rice."

"I shall be Ling Wa's shield," Kwok assured.

A harvester named Ming Lo asked, "Why wouldn't The Idiot choose one of his own?"

"Who would take him?" Lao Shu replied.

As promised, Kwok trailed Ling Wa like a suitor. He was accompanied by his prized ghetto blaster, from which he listened to a collection of classic rock 'n' roll CDs.

"Who," he asked Ling Wa, "is your favourite singer? Mine is Little Richard."

While the girl had heard of Madonna, she knew nothing of this Mr. Little. She grew fond of Kwok's musical preferences, however, and her gentle palladium. Out on the clam beds, the ghetto blaster at full volume, the pair would ape the popular dances of the sixties.

A-wop-bop-a-loo-lop . . .

The refrain skimmed across the beach, scattering the sandpipers.

"It's called Tutti Frutti," said Kwok.

. . . *a-lop-bam-boo!*

A snorting congregation of seals sunning themselves on the rocky point appeared bemused. The elders shook their heads and resumed digging.

Seven days a week, from early morning until darkness drove them from the clam beds, the harvesters gathered the heart-shaped cockle, an elusive mollusk that uses its tiny legs to burrow deep into the sand. This meaty creature, the panel learned, was coveted by well-heeled diners the world over. On special occasions the diggers would smuggle a batch into camp. Be Shing would marinate the tasty shellfish in vinegar, serving them raw.

Each digger carried a white plastic container deep enough to bathe an infant. When several had been filled with cockles, The Idiot steered an all-terrain vehicle onto the clam beds and loaded them onto a trailer. He distributed empties and tallied the numbers in a notebook.

Sometimes Kwok would insert the ghetto blaster into one of the empties; he liked the way it made the sound carry.

"Could someone get to the point?" asked a panelist.

"Recently," explained Diane Ng, "many countries concerned about overharvesting have imposed moratoriums. This has caused the price to increase here. These people are experienced diggers in their home country. They work long hours and for much less than our minimum wage."

The widow Lao Shu took up the story. Apprehensive addressing strangers in imperfect English, she asked Diane Ng to assist.

"Andrew knew we wouldn't complain about being shortchanged. If the camp was discovered, we'd lose everything. We don't have passports; he owned us. When we are returned to our country, we will be punished and fined. The money will be shared by the police and the judge. Those of us who cannot pay will be jailed or forced into servitude. By comparison, your prison is a holiday resort."

"The facility where you're being housed," one of the panelists corrected, "is a *holding* centre. It's state-of-the-art."

"Perhaps," conceded Lao Shu. "But the doors are still locked, and our jailers are holding the keys."

Others confirmed that though working conditions for the harvesters were difficult, poaching was still lucrative. It was particularly demanding for someone as slight as Ling Wa, who, in the altogether, weighed less than a container full of cockles.

"Most of us," reported another, "earn in a month what we'd make in a year back home."

One harvester said his remuneration supported a family of eight. A son was attending teacher's college.

"What I don't understand," he asked Diane Ng to convey, "is why we are being held, and why all this talk? The recruiters, our thieving boss, the restaurant owners, the patrons — they're not in your holding centre."

The court was told the harvesters were paid in cash at the end of each week. Sums were secured in a strongbox watched over by Be Shing.

During the break a reporter leaned over the railing and asked Lao Shu if the detainees' families were aware of their predicament.

"How could they know?" she replied. "Most of our families don't have telephones. Some of us can't read or write in our own language."

"Does it surprise you," pressed the reporter, "that those responsible for smuggling you into this country are not being sought?"

"No," said Lao Shu. "Haven't you been listening? We are — how do you say? — in-wiz-i-bo."

"Do you mean," asked the reporter, "*invisible?*"

"Exac-wee," said Lao Shu. "In-wiz-i-bo."

Out on the beach, sunbeams refracting off the unfurling waves, gulls keening overhead, Kwok switched on the ghetto blaster. It wasn't often he played the traditional favourites. Each note plucked on the ancient instrument wafted on the brackish ocean breeze.

"Ahh . . . " said one of the harvesters, recognizing the music.

At the conclusion of the first selection, some of the women wiped tears from their cheeks. The lyrics spoke of young lovers long ago. The old timers straightened up, their hooded eyes fixed on a spot along the horizon whence all had come and to where all longed to return.

"Do you miss your home?" Ling Wa asked Lao Shu.

The widow was watching a blue heron wade into a tide pool and spear lunch. She was wondering why humans had such difficulty feeding themselves.

"Even with its many imperfections," she replied. "I miss my homeland every day. Every minute."

Because of Kwok's omnipresence, Willy transferred his attentions to a newcomer, Song Lee, a wife and mother.

"What does The Idiot see in Song Lee?" an elder had asked. "She's not nearly as pretty as Ling Wa."

"Large breasts," replied another. "Ling Wa's are the size of pears." The elders studied them as Ling Wa stepped from the shower.

"When a man sees such things, he loses his senses."

Because of her years, but mostly because she was keeper of the strongbox, Be Shing was afforded the last word.

"The most beautiful breasts," said the mother of ten, thrusting forward a drooping bosom, "are those that produce the most milk."

The elders hastily reassigned Kwok to watch over Song Lee. Kwok was saddened by the request. During his term as Ling Wa's protector, they had become each other's Tutti Frutti.

Ling Wa explained through the translator that Willy had become enraged at her friendship with Kwok. With the young harvester guarding Song Lee, Willy was free to resume the abuse. His fingers would tear like feeding crabs at her clothing.

"Stuck-up little slant," he snarled. "Be nice!"

Ling Wa resisted as best she could.

"Another time," she said, "I was at the stream, washing up."

She halted her testimony abruptly and hung her head. Back home, one didn't speak of such things, and certainly not in public.

A full moon bathed the weary harvesters as they trudged across the sand. Most had almost filled their quota for the month. Out on the point the waves tumbled lazily onto the shoreline, breaking open on the rocks and throwing up spray.

The Crown map on display at the hearing referred to this place as Wentworth Inlet. It was named after a British admiral who had surveyed these waters. To the Indians who lived here, this place had always been the Bay of Noisy Gulls. Crown literature stating otherwise was considered a durable toilet tissue.

The wind that night picked up, and the sea began to roil and pitch. Billowing clouds intercepted the moon. One minute the harvesters could make out the ATV on shore, Shep gambolling, and then they couldn't see each other. It began to rain, a frigid horizontal lashing.

A Fisheries official explained what happened next.

"These bays and inlets can fill in via tide streams that enter obliquely. The mist and fog limit visibility; the harvesters would have no way of knowing what was going on in their rear. By the time they did, they could be stranded on a dissolving sandbar kilometres from shore."

A panelist asked, "Isn't someone responsible for alerting the group?"

"Spotters on shore typically sound the alarm."

That would be Andrew and Willy, who had taken advantage of the darkness to race back to camp and pry open the strongbox, the price of shellfish having dropped precipitously. Be Shing tried stopping them, but Shep lunged at her. The old woman was recuperating

40

in hospital. Her translated affidavit, already read aloud, corroborated the others.

The harvesters told the court of the sea coming at them from both directions. About how the hard-packed sand turned to jelly underfoot. Many became disoriented and headed out to sea — to their deaths. Ling Wa stumbled to shore, hypothermic.

"We carried a change of clothes," she said. "Some aboriginals built a fire. I was helped out of my wet things and given hot tea."

Another wept while recounting the pleading of co-workers caught by the tide.

"Anyone who didn't reach shore in the first few minutes was lost. The current was very strong. The natives used their boats to bring some of the bodies ashore. They stayed with us through the night, banging drums and chanting. If it wasn't for them, more would have perished. They didn't eat anyone."

The storm passed, and the moon reclaimed its eminence in the sky. Survivors rushed to the water's edge to search for stragglers, but none were found. Beyond the point the survivors could make out a fleet of the white containers, the current sweeping them out to open sea. Ling Wa told the inquiry that between the thump of waves pounding the shoreline she had heard something else as well.

A-wop-bop-a-loo-lop, Mr. Little was carolling, *a-lop-bam-boo . . .*

Sweet & Sour

THE BOTTOM OF THE ELEVATOR SHAFT, TOWARDS which our protagonist plunges, has for years served as a boneyard to the hapless and the deserving. We don't want Milan Kobek, the Chechen gang leader, brushing himself off just yet, so let's snap a leg and bruise a few ribs . . . He regains consciousness as a flashlight's snoopy beam is auditing his crippled remains.

"Still breathing, Kobek?"

The voice comes from the third floor of the derelict warehouse where, moments earlier, Kobek felt a pair of hands on his back, a nudge. Its tone and inflection are familiar to him, but he is immobilized with pain and unable to identify the speaker.

"That the money there beside ya?"

Kobek sweeps an arm out to one side. The satchel, containing the proceeds of the heist, has preserved his skull. But his cellphone, and with it any opportunity to summon reinforcements, has, like his leg, shattered on impact.

"I'm gonna toss down a rope. Attach the bag to it, hear? Don't make me come and get it."

The gang leader feigns termination.

"You pass up the money," says the voice, unconvinced, "and I'll get a doctor."

Kobek hadn't risen to prominence in the underworld accepting assurances without collateral. He likes to tell his crew that promises are like wicker furniture and fat women: the former are easily disabled by the latter.

Despite blood pooling into his eyes, he can make out dust motes dancing through a ray of light. He can hear pigeons flapping indignant wings.

Upon conviction of money laundering and assault with a deadly weapon, Milan Kobek had been advised that, while incarcerated, he would be wise to attend group therapy sessions and self-help courses, of which, in today's penal system, there is a generous menu. Parole boards, he was told, view submission favourably.

"Of course it's bullshit," said his lawyer. "It's lapdogs who sit on parole boards. But you best toss them something to chew on."

The Chechen refused, and as a consequence endured the full term of his sentence. He also declined to declare Christ his personal saviour, a common but rarely successful inmate calculation. The only creed Kobek adhered to was this: first there is betrayal, then retribution.

To commemorate his liberation after four years in the penitentiary, his associates threw a party at a swanky downtown hotel. Rival warlords — a temporary truce was customary — praised his defiance. Afterwards, two of the city's finest whores were delivered to his suite.

In the morning, Hong, a trusted lieutenant, joined him in the coffee shop.

"While you were away, boss, some of the others have been sharpening their knives. Guys you thought were friends."

There was also the matter of Frankie Choo. Gangs conduct their business like nations: they remain within designated demarcations, most of the time. Problem was, Hong explained, while Kobek was in the slammer, Frankie and his Red Dragons had been muscling in on neighbouring enterprises.

Though some of the boys were apoplectic that Hong — a Yellow, they called him — had been allowed on the team, Kobek ignored their objections. He'd needed someone who knew the way of the Red Dragons. In the Chechen's absence, their noodle shops had spread like a head cold.

"All that meth, Frankie's hard to figure, boss," Hong said. "He might be somebody else's problem now. We do nothing, he becomes ours."

This was corroborated by other sources, each of whom urged that someone step up and burn Frankie before a turf war erupted. As the longest surviving leader, Kobek accepted the responsibility. But first he had another score to settle.

Fast Eddie Meeker was what wise guys referred to as pocket lint. He supplied info and swapped favours — whatever was necessary to fill his next spike. The biggest mistake he ever made — let's have Eddie exiting a restaurant, whistling down a cab — was ratting out Milan Kobek.

The cops had nabbed Eddie in a sting; he was looking at a lengthy bit. The offer? A Get-Out-Of-Jail card in exchange for everything he had on the Chechen. Eddie didn't figure he had much choice.

"Drop me off anywhere near there," he tells the cabbie, a Turban. Eddie wants to fix before joining a pal at The Cellar, a jazz club. A lot of peelers hang out there after the taverns close, and Eddie has a thing for peelers.

At the crest of a bridge the cab pulls over. It's a secondary route into town and traffic that time of night is sparse. The Turban jumps out, runs to the rail and unzips.

Faint with the sickness, Eddie rolls down the window.

"We ain't on no curry farm in the Punjab!" he hollers.

"Very sorry, sir." The cabbie giggles. "Bapu makes water."

Eddie has a length of pipe he wants to try out, so he slips from the back seat and crosses the road. But before he can take a swing, Bapu turns.

"Remember me, Eddie?" The turban and whiskers rest at their feet.

"You!"

A gelatinous goo connected to a spine was found floating in the harbour a few days later. The pilot of a passenger ferry had heard a thud. The cops wrote it up as a jumper.

There was a wave of drive-bys that summer, just as Hong had predicted. The newspapers were reporting unidentified human remains being dumped, diced, buried or, in one case, still smouldering. Bits and pieces were washing up on popular swimming beaches.

"We think we know who's responsible," the city's police chief told the press. "The task force has been beefed up."

He didn't say what many suspected: that as long as thugs knocked off thugs, the police would look the other way. Taxpayers were quietly thankful.

With Frankie Choo the probable catalyst, Kobek's recruitment of Hong now seemed prescient. Nevertheless, some of the soldiers, especially the older ones, continued griping.

"We don't trust the Yellows," said one longtime associate, "and they don't trust us."

But Kobek had a soft spot for the Canton native, and an appetite for sweet and sour anything, the reason the gang met at the Golden Wok. Despite growling stomachs — there was much to discuss, and the assembly was dragging on — the stubborn amongst them refused to sample the unfamiliar dishes spread out before them. One soldier used his chopstick to dissect a dumpling. Another scrutinized a fish ball and called for a spoon — cancelling the request when the others moaned their disapproval.

Kobek reminded his grumbling troops of Hong's first assignment, a haberdasher with an overdue loan. The new enforcer was asked for proof he'd visited the man's shop, a standard request of an untested recruit. Others would have turned over to the boss whatever cash was in the register.

"You recall how Hong handled the matter?" Kobek asked. "He turned over a wad of bills . . . and the poor bugger's thumb. We had the balance inside a week."

Kobek was also a sucker for an adventure story. Hong's escape from China reminded him of the tales his grandfather told of the last big war in Europe. Hong and a cousin crossed an estuary clinging to an inner tube. A shark appeared. Hong made it to shore. His cousin didn't.

"Why should we believe you?" queried one of the boys. "I saw that movie."

Hong hoisted a pant leg. Everybody leaned in for a look-see. The scar extended from the ankle to mid-thigh.

Kobeck arranged a confab with Chico Fernandez, the ruler of Los Diablos. They met in neutral territory, a poolroom on Kingsway.

"You wan me to take out Frankie?" the Dominican said. "No problemo, Milan. I never like that guy."

The Diablos kingpin snacked on sunflower seeds. Shells covered the floor like bullet casings after a reckoning. He had something of the sewer about him. Word was that he practised voodoo, which didn't bother Kobek. Wops practised Catholicism.

"Gang leaders are like diapers," said Fernandez, who'd recently authored a successful putsch against his own. "They should be changed often."

"You and Frankie have an arrangement," Kobek reminded him. "It gonna bother you switching sides, Chico?"

"We did some things together," Fernandez acknowledged. "But all your friends become enemies if you live long enough. Looking for loyalty in this business is like looking for a turtle with a moustache."

Deliberations dragged on through the afternoon and into the evening. Fernandez was holding out for a massage parlour; with Frankie Choo out of the way, A Touch of Class would revert to Kobek. The Los Diablos warlord was sweet on one of the girls there, an enormous Rwandan Tutsi named Choco.

Blunts were circulated and bottles drained. There were toasts to the new allegiance, to integrity and longevity, to everyone's mother.

Finally Kobek relented.

"Okay," he told Chico. "We have a deal."

Frankie Choo was found at the wheel of his Porsche, a single bullet in the temple. Kills talk to those who listen, and this one said: Ain't gonna break a sweat roughing you up, Frankie. Ain't gonna waste a second bullet. Sunflower seed shells and a lone copper casing below the driver's window suggested the killer stuck around a while, savouring the moment.

Meanwhile (as storytellers are fond of saying), at the bottom of the elevator shaft, Kobek is stirred by a racket from above. The sound of brick separating from brick, of wood from wood, the hiss of matter soaring through dead air. Something joins him at the bottom of the shaft.

Kobek assumes construction material tossed into the shaft by a man impatient for the satchel. But then it sighs. Kobek opens his eyes.

"I don't believe it!"

One side of Hong's face is already beginning to swell.

"Nothing personal, boss. Just business."

"All that I did for your career? I shoulda listened to the boys."

Kobek attempts to swat Hong, but he crawls out of reach.

"Let me explain . . . "

"I don't want to hear it! We're both finished."

"My sister's baby is sick . . . "

"I don't give a — "

"The runt needs surgery. It's not like here."

Hong unknots his necktie and rigs a sling for his shattered arm. Kobek offers him a Demerol, a habit he picked up in the joint. He always packs a vial for such eventualities.

"Take it. You might as well leave this world with a smile on your face."

Of all his underlings, Hong is the last Kobek would suspect of treachery. The man who dog-paddled to freedom must, like himself, have entered the life reluctantly, a victim of circumstance.

"Anybody in this with you?"

Hong names a few others upset by their share of the spoils. Of promotions denied and slights unforgiven.

They include those who'd called for Hong's ouster. It's another lesson Kobek learns: when coups are hatched, plotters are colour-blind.

"They should arrive any minute," Hong says.

"If my guys show first," Kobek returns, "you're rat food."

What the gang leader said next might have been playing the odds. Or it could have been a softening that appears with age — a need for atonement. The Demerol likely had something to do with it.

"I say we have an armistice," Kobek says.

"You're always using big words, boss."

"If my boys arrive first, we drop you at the hospital. Your guys get here before mine, you do likewise for me."

But Hong falls silent, and Kobek notices for the first time blood leaking from the Chinaman. In the fading light it expands like an oil spill.

"Agreed," Hong finally says.

Kobek slides the satchel to Hong.

"Either way," he says. "You take the cash. For the kid."

Our story concludes with rain drumming on the roof of the warehouse.

"Listen!" Kobek says. "You hear that?"

"It's probably just the wind, boss."

At the sound of voices, both stiffen.

"Our deal still good?" Kobek asks.

"You have my word."

"Hello down there!"

Flakes fall like volcano ash through the stale, dank air of the elevator shaft. Whatever it is brushes their faces and snags in their hair.

"Must be bird crap," Kobek says.

Let's say a demolition crew finds the bodies and calls the cops. Let's say both corpses wear a smile. An empty vial is found at the scene, but there is no satchel, no money. The officer processing the scene, a rookie, doesn't think the sunflower seed shells worth mentioning in his report. Kills talk, but only to those who know the language.

Green Honda

ARCHIE SPOTTED THE SCANNER AT A SWAP meet. The hawker evidently concluded that he wasn't an undercover cop, because he leaned across the pile of swag and said, "It's your lucky day, buddy."

Lila dismissed the scanner, about the size of Archie's shoe, as "just another stupid toy."

Once he got the hang of things, though, Archie was eavesdropping on firefighters and paramedics, on the banter of security guards, construction crews, and bicycle couriers. But the hawker had been right: the police frequency was best.

After dinner most nights, Lila's fanny parked in front of the flat screen, he'd lie in bed, the lights out, listening to police working stakeouts and drug busts, in pursuit of robbery suspects and car thieves.

The action was unedited and often profane.

Atmospheric interference sometimes made dialogue unintelligible. But when the sky was clear and the night air crisp, his evenings were high drama. The ticketing of teen dragsters and the separation of feuding couples. The search for peeping Toms, cat burglars, and fugitives.

Reality radio. Of course he couldn't *see* the "perps," as the police called them. It was like listening to one of those taped books for the sightless: you had to imagine the cast of characters.

He did research. The police wore a small microphone clipped to their lapels. So refined was the technology that he could discern the pounding of a heart or a constable slurping coffee, every burp, every groan, every sigh. You could visualize cigarette smoke ebbing from lungs after a take down.

The overlap of voices could be confusing, but in time he began to recognize the officers consigned to the evening shift. The cast lead was a senior detective, a Scot named McPherson who referred to cop and criminal alike as "laddie." There were several Scots on the force, but Archie could always identify McPherson because he could hear the stem of a tobacco pipe rattling between his teeth.

"Patience, lad," the detective counselled a rookie. "People don't just up and vanish. It might take a while, but sooner or later we'll catch the bugger."

He'd brought home the scanner a few weeks after the honeymoon — a weekend in Vegas, a Shopping Channel stone on Lila's finger. Within a few months he knew the marriage wouldn't survive. It was the way Lila rolled her eyes when he recounted an incident at work.

"Then this customer says to me . . . "

But she wasn't listening. Lila didn't appreciate the sacrifices he made to afford those sushi dinners on the west side. Women, Archie believed, weren't programmed to appreciate what men did for them.

"A fella still godda have da hole he can call his own," said his boss Myron, of Myron's Meats, following Lila's exit. "Da home port." Myron would only broach the subject when Marlina, his own of several decades, was away from the shop on errands.

Myron was a European from a town Archie couldn't pronounce. He had mossy forearms sturdy as a length of timber. Ten years earlier he had come to the vocational school looking for an apprentice meat cutter. Instructors recommended the young Archibald Louie because of his dexterity with the cleavers.

"Vy dey call you dat?" Myron had asked at the job interview. His accent could be as thick as a sausage. "Vy Jop Louie?"

"Ever eat Chinese?" Archie replied. "Dish they call chop suey? I can juggle the cleavers like bowling pins, never a nick."

"Do you believe in trade unions?" Myron inquired.

Who in that class didn't believe in unions? All were aware that a member of the local chapter could earn double that of someone working for an independent.

"Isn't that, like, communism?" Archie answered.

He started work the following Monday.

With Lila out of the picture Archie could listen to the scanner at any hour, in any room, its crackle and screech be damned. He also had the time and resources to launch the home business he'd always dreamed of, Archie's Fine

Meats. He'd been in the industry long enough to realize that ownership was the only way to make any real money.

Myron had made it clear when he hired Archie that he didn't want to train someone only to see him quit and become a competitor. He had promised Myron he'd never do such a thing.

He purchased a freezer from a retiring butcher and cleaned out the garage. He bought wholesale and sold evenings and weekends — only quality cuts. Once word got around, demand for Archie's products quickly exceeded supply. The most popular item was a stew made from leftovers, a concoction flavoured with garlic and ginger. It was so unlike what most carnivores were accustomed to that everyone expressed curiosity about the ingredients.

"Top secret," Archie would say.

Only a few of his customers were poached from the shop. Folks he'd developed a relationship with over the years, people he could trust not to squeal to Myron, who'd surely sack him were he to learn of the betrayal.

Even so, he began to fear Myron suspected something. Hadn't his employer been distant recently? On the drive home from work one evening Archie also noticed a car, a green Honda, following his pickup. A private spook?

But his employer was too tight for such an extravagance. And what if Myron did discover his sideline? Free country, ain't it?

At a bankruptcy sale he bought cabinets, tubs, a cast-iron stewing vat, a gleaming new set of cutlery. When, after a night of work, he swung open the garage doors to hose the detritus into the sewers, the freshly rinsed blades sparkled like dewdrops in the morning light.

Like so many men of his temperament, he was happiest at labour — in his case, bent over a carcass, separating the edible from bone and gristle, the blood pooling around his rubber boots.

Chop Louie.

"Online dating," Myron was saying. "You can look at da picture first. Turn off dat damn scanner."

But Archie couldn't locate a computer's power switch. And he balked at the idea of another spouse so soon after Lila. Which didn't stop Myron from raising the subject whenever Marlina ventured beyond hearing range.

"Who vas dat dame you took to da pictures? Before Lila."

Myron was excising fat from a rump of roast, wrapping the raw slab in a sheet of wax paper.

"You know," Myron said. "Wit da boobs?"

"They all have 'em," Archie said. "Two each, usually."

"Dis big?"

"Sonia."

"Dats da one!"

They had the same conversation every few months. *Vat ever happen to da one with da boobs?* Sonia worked at a bakery in a nearby mall; Archie had taken her to a Clint Eastwood movie. When he tried kissing her afterwards, Sonia offered cheek.

"She got back together with an old boyfriend," Archie lied.

Archie sometimes returned to the same mall where he'd met Sonia; it was on his route home. He'd pretend interest in an item to win the attention of some clerk who'd caught his eye. If he was drawn to one he'd make a purchase just to lengthen the encounter. He was drawn to a woman's scent. Not the perfume, her.

"Come to think of it," he might say, "I could use some of those . . . "

Leaving the mall one evening, walking through the underground lot, Archie sensed someone observing him from a parked car. He tried getting a better look in his rearview mirror, but the lighting was poor. Of the colour and make of vehicle he was certain: it was a green Honda.

When he could work up the nerve, times when loneliness throbbed like an infection, Archie visited the whores. He unwisely confided this to Myron, who insisted on knowing how much and for how long.

And exactly vat did von get, huh?

Archie slid a book of matches across the counter. The cover featured a busty brunette whose blouse opened when held up to the light. Knockers, the club was called, an all-night strip joint and cabaret. He'd met Lila there. For fifty dollars she'd spent twenty minutes with him in a room at the Regent Motel. Before the wedding she'd been keen.

Myron held the book of matches up to the window. When he heard Marlina's car backfire out back, he slid the contraband under the cash register.

"Next time da vife takes holiday in da Old Country," he winked, "we go togedder."

Archie could sense something was wrong when he dropped by the shop to pick up his paycheque. Marlina's greeting was muted, and Myron refused to acknowledge his presence. With the CLOSED sign posted in the window, the two men alone, Myron got right to the point.

"How long you been vorking privately, huh? Vat da matter? Day job not good enuff?"

Archie felt certain Myron was responsible for the Honda. How else could he have known about Archie's Fine Meats? But his employer insisted a lady had visited the shop; she told him about Archie's stew.

"Your vork here," Myron said, "is finisht."

A week later Marlina calls him at home.

"Dat bastard!" she snivels. "Dat son-of-a-bitch!"

She tells Archie about the squabble. Myron had sped off in the van. She hadn't seen him in three days.

"So I start looking around for da clue," she says. "I find under da cash register."

The matchbook from Knockers. Marlina is convinced Myron is shacked up with a whore.

"Dat dog!"

Archie agrees to return to work temporarily. A month stretches into three, then six. After about a year, no sign of the eponymous proprietor, Marlina tells Archie she doesn't miss Myron all that much. She changes the name of the business to Marlina's Meats. Sometimes she invites

Archie over to the house for a plate of liverwurst. He always brings a batch of stew.

Archie switches on the scanner one night just as the police are closing in on a suspect. Between sharp bursts of static, the conversation truncated, he's able to surmise that the culprit lives nearby. He has resided in the neighbourhood for years; he wonders who it might be.

"Our people are in position."

The Scot, McPherson.

"Proceed with caution, lads." The stem of the policeman's pipe is rattling around in his mouth. "This guy's a piece of work."

The lights dimmed, his eyes closed, Archie fancies a badge pinned to his breast, strapping on a bulletproof vest, a revolver heavy as a brick nestled in his perspiring palm.

"On three!" McPherson says.

Archie bounds from bed and peeks out the window. Police cruisers, their emergency lights casting a crimson glow, block both ends of the street. Neighbours in pajamas gather like crows on the front lawn.

Then he sees it.

At the curb.

A green Honda.

He cranks up the volume on the scanner. He hears a door being wrenched from its hinges. He switches off the scanner and hears a stampede of heavy boots in the hallway.

Rapture

GIMME A BREAK, GIMME FIVE, GIMME A burger and chips. Gimme the benefit of the doubt, gimme one last chance or, hey, just gimme a blowjob. In the group home they instruct the boys never to say gimme. Mrs. McDermott ladles out the fruit juice, singing, *Gimme gimme never gets.* The boys have to sing it or they don't get any. But it's Lonnie's first day; he doesn't know the drill. Get fucked, he says. I'm not singin'. That's when he's introduced to Mr. McDermott's fist. Lonnie's disappearance is discovered in the morning, it being Wednesday, and Wednesday being change-the-sheets day. In his place is Dolly, the McDermotts' cat, Mr. McDermott's bootlace cinched around its neck.

It's late on a Saturday night. The rain hasn't let up for days. Lonnie's in an alley across from the station; he's been on a Rapture binge. If he doesn't get more soon things are gonna get nasty. A westbound train arrives, a recorded voice announcing, *Collingwood, next stop, Collingwood.*

He ducks into a doorwell, leans his skateboard against the wall. Passengers dissipate into the night. A few make for the alley. An elderly couple huddled under an umbrella passes; pot-smoking teens trail. Earlier, Sweet called him on his cell. Get over to Rubin's, she says, 'cause Howie Bowles is bringing the stuff. Lonnie has never met Howie Bowles, but who gives a? His R is righteous and the price is right. Nothing else matters. Absolutely nothing.

I'm crashing, lover, Sweet says. She was the captain of her high school basketball team, a beauty once. Get here fast, she pleads. Ah, Sweet. Get up, get down, get a grip. We'll get high, then we'll get it on. Sweet's parents once persuaded her to check into rehab, some five-star facility. She said it was like walking through the pages of *People* magazine, all the surgically altered faces.

A straggler appears at the head of the alley. He's humming along to a tune on his iPod. Real smart of you, fool: dark alley, head down, earbuds. You should hang a sign around your neck, saying, Mug me, I'm stupid. Lonnie steps from a shadow, taps Stupid on the shoulder.

Gimme everything . . .

You can ingest it, snort it, spike it or shove it up your ass. Whatever the preference, Rapture swoops into the bloodstream like a hurricane making landfall. The rush starts with a tingling along the soles of the feet before it climbs up the shin bones, sweeps over the kneecaps, explores like lustful fingers the inside of the thighs. Then it creeps up the torso and branches off to the arms, the fingertips, to the raw lining of the throat. When it reaches the scalp, there being no place else to go, R delivers a wallop to the cerebral cortex that can trigger a convulsion. Good shit can make a boy whimper.

When he got busted the first time, intent to traffic, Lonnie was sentenced to three months. His first day inside a con says to him, Whattya need, fish? Ain't nothin' we don't got, and he wasn't lyin'. The second time he got busted, a possession rap, he was sent to rehab for twenty-eight days. A few weeks into the program he says to his caseworker, No more, I swear, man, and the next thing he knows they've reduced his sentence by ten days, good behaviour. Tell the do-gooders you're going to finish high school, that you've got a job lined up, they swoon. It don't matter that it's all bullshit.

The thing about rehab is that those running the place don't know Rapture. They might know the other stuff out there — AC/DC, Bang, Blue Devils — and some might even be ex-users, but of R, most know only rumours. Drug counsellors are like Sunday school teachers: they go by the book, no questions asked. If you don't change your ways, they say, you'll die. Do you want to die? They just don't get it. The people they're talking to, people like Lonnie James, already have.

So what does Lonnie do the day he's released? Calls Sweet, of course. I need you, girl, he tells her. Got any? What else is a dope-sick boy to do? Where's he going to go? Bowling? Choir practice?

Lonnie sold prescription meds from a corner on Hastings Street; it was the only job he'd ever had. He and Sweet lived in a squat, the top floor of a condemned building. It was nice in summer, cool, you could smell the ocean, but there was no heat, so winters there were a lot like alpine camping. You crawled in through the window and the cockroaches scattered like urchins caught stripping a BMW. High, though, the squat was a penthouse, the Shangri-freaking-la.

Lonnie hops onto his board and surfs the length of Wellington Road. He enters Rubin's house through the back door. Rubin rests his shaggy head on the kitchen table. Sweet's in a bad way. She sits, she stands, she sits again. Then she scoots down the hallway like she's late to a meeting. Every couple of minutes she's back at the living room window. Is it him? she asks. Is it Howie? A car door slams, a passerby coughs, she's launching an investigation.

He'll be here any sec, Rubin says, Howie's a professional. Then he starts pacing, a panther in a cage. His cell rings while he's in the other room; Lonnie picks up. It's Petra, Rubin's girl, mother of their boy Josh, a sullen twig of a thing who's filling in a colouring book. Petra serves drinks at some dive downtown. Like everybody else, she's crashing. She's on her break, working her sources. So far, she tells Lonnie, no luck, the town's dry. Tell Rubin to feed the kid, will ya? While he's still fucking able.

There's a girl named Luba in the back room. She's sick, too, and won't come out until Howie shows. Luba's always changing her hairdo. She's been a blond, a redhead, a bluehead. Tonight she's a skinhead. Rubin says some rap singer has written a song about her. It was on the radio; he heard it.

Luba often says things Lonnie doesn't understand, things like, It's easy to be wise. Just think of something stupid to say, then don't say it. Another time she claimed to be an artist. Let's see some of your work, Lonnie said. Wanna see some of my poetry? she asked. No thanks, Lonnie said. But I'd really like to see your tits.

Lonnie dipped into his emergency stash earlier, so he's in better shape than the others. But if he loves Sweet as much as he professes, why not ease her discomfort? Of course I love her . . . but not *that* much. Besides, if Sweet knew about the emergency stash, there wouldn't be an emergency stash. That's the way things work: if you can steal it, the stuff is yours, fair and square. Love? It's just a word, man.

He microwaves a tin of soup, the only grub in the house, and serves it to Josh. The kid is so hungry he licks the empty bowl.

Here's how it went down in the alley: Stupid tells Lonnie to piss off, because he's not giving nothing to nobody, especially some snot-dripping dope freak. Big mistake to tell some snot-dripping dope freak who's crashing to piss off. It also signals there's something in the backpack worth protecting. The first blow drops Stupid and shatters the iPod, but the hammer is wet and it flies out of Lonnie's hand. He reaches for the skateboard and starts whacking the guy until he can't whack no more.

Another train approaches just as he's dragging the body into the doorwell. *Collingwood, next stop, Collingwood.* Lonnie rifles through the guy's pockets, finds about $200. He's unzipping the backpack when Stupid opens his eyes, looks up at Lonnie, a long positive-ID kind of look.

Commuters are streaming into the alley, their footsteps clacking on the pavement. Three more blows of the skateboard and Stupid slumps over. Shoulda played dead, fool; now you can't play at all. Lonnie grabs his board and slips in behind the commuters. Stupid's hat is in the gutter; it's raining harder than ever, so he scoops it up. Rob's Break & Wheel, it says on the brim. The 'o' in Rob is a tire with spokes. Lonnie almost reached Rubin's place when he realized he didn't finish searching the backpack.

Luba emerges from hibernation and giddy-ups to the bathroom. The first person to use up their stuff is always the first to heave; it's like Newton's Law. Lonnie suspects Sweet will be next. Rubin calls everybody into the living room and ignites a spliff; it helps with the headaches, but only for a few minutes. Howie should be here any minute now, Rubin assures. Petra comes home, we'll order some wings.

Next time Lonnie checks the clock on the wall thirty minutes have disappeared, and there's still no sign of Howie. That's the thing about R. It's not that time goes fast or slow; it's irrelevant. The only one in the house who couldn't care less about Howie Bowles is steering a plastic fire truck across the floor. He's singing a song from Sesame Street.

A frantic Luba tells them to come quick — blood is seeping out from under the bathroom door. Rubin and Lonnie find Sweet on her knees, a crimson spray bubbling from her wrist, the razor blade still imbedded in the artery. Forgive me, baby, she says to Lonnie, I just can't do this anymore. Rubin dials 911. Josh observes from the hallway. The expression on his face says it all: I've seen this cartoon before, Daddy.

The paramedics squeeze into the bathroom with Sweet and close the door. Then the police show up. They enter everyone's name into a laptop, which tells them what they want to know. Sweet isn't looking too good when they wheel her out on a stretcher. Petra turns up soon after the uniforms split. She's scored. They gather around the kitchen table like it's a birthday party and time for cake. Rubin tightens a length of tubing around his left arm; a vein the length of a garden worm rises to the surface of his bicep.

Later, everybody nodding off, Luba comments on Lonnie's new hat. That's weird, she says. Howie's got a hat looks just like yours: Rob's Brake & Wheel, the spokes . . . Looks like rain. Looks like an Egyptian. Luba's lips are moving, but Lonnie can't make out what she's saying. Because he's hurtling through the universe faster than the speed of sound, faster than a beam of light, a dumb-assed grin splashed across his dumb face.

Mothas

SEE THAT CRAWLSPACE BENEATH THE SCHOOL portable? Two kids prying loose a plank and squeezing inside? And those overturned crates ringing a firepit? When school is out, as it is today, Mothas like Bugs call it the Party Palace.

— My feet are soaked, he says.

— I need a cig, says 8-Ball. Want one?

Candle stubs poke from empty liquor bottles. They ignite three.

— You sure brought enough stuff, Bugs says. Like his carrot-nibbling namesake, Bugs has prominent central incisors.

They study each other's luggage: 8-Ball's suitcase wrestled shut by a length of belt, Bugs' gym bag.

— Think your folks will call the cops? 8-Ball asks.

— My old man won't. He hasn't said a word since the plant closed.

There's enough scrap wood for a small fire. Bugs peels off his wet socks, gives them a squeeze, holds them over the nascent blaze. One year later a partying Motha will torch the Palace. He'll be sniffing glue when he concludes he's being held captive inside an iceberg. Had to melt it, he'll convince the others. Had to break free.

— We're sitting directly under Laura Sauder's desk, says 8-Ball. He's been smitten with the girl since kindergarten, the way she glides along the halls at school, celestial. He enshrined their initials in wet cement, carved them into a picnic table.

— She the one with the jugs?

— I'd give anything to see them.

Bugs toes 8-Ball's suitcase.

— Good. You might wanna lighten your load.

— If we had X-ray vision, says 8-Ball, and if school was in, we could see her panties.

Each quietly considers the advantages of such a power.

— Titties are for milking, Bugs says.

Through a crack in the wall the boys look out over the playing field, a patch of mud and weed pockmarked by soccer cleats and tire tracks. The ruts have filled with rainwater.

— Maybe she doesn't wear panties, Bugs says. Ever think of that?

8-Ball has. Many times.

A freight train rumbles alongside the schoolyard most afternoons. Mothas ambush the rusty leviathan with stones and bottles, a blow against the forces enslaving them. Housewives rely on the train's passing as a reminder to start the vegetables.

— I like it when they don't wear bras, 8-Ball says. You can't actually see them, but you know they're there.

Mothas

— I like the hole best, says Bugs. The hole is home.

— I haven't seen one of those yet, 8-Ball says. Not for real, up close.

But for the magazines an older brother stashes under his bed, neither has Bugs.

They flick their cigarettes outside and light two more.

Three thumps on the Palace wall — the signal — and Pete squeezes inside. Pete lives with his mom and her boyfriend, the biker Caleb Stark, who everybody knows has been to jail and has a tattoo of a snake. Pete's possessions are stuffed into two plastic shopping bags.

— Mothas . . .

— Where's —

— Ain't coming.

— What about —

— He didn't want to miss lacrosse practice. His team made the finals.

— They're not real Mothas, Bugs declares.

— Weekenders, 8-Ball agrees.

Pete unbuttons his mackinaw jacket; an assortment of shoplifted snacks tumbles to the ground.

— Get any Ding Dongs? 8-Ball asks.

— Chang's son was working in the store today, Pete says. He wouldn't take his eyes off me.

— Smart guy, says Bugs.

The Changs own Eastside Market & Produce. After school, kids swarm its aisles.

— I heard they're from China, 8-Ball says. They know kung fu, even grandma.

69

— They're not from China, Bugs says. They're from Shanghai.

— Quiet! Pete says. You guys hear something?

They take turns peeking through the crack in the wall. To the east are the woods, dark and still. In every other direction it's shingled rooftops and drooping telephone lines. An occasional treetop, like a loose strand of hair, peeks above the chimneys.

What they hear is just the rain, rain and wind making mischief in the poplar trees. And them, three adolescents on the day of their emancipation.

A gull drops from a light pole and struts through the mud. A math test — a fail — gambols across the field, slamming into a chain-link fence.

— I brought Elaine Brenner here once, Pete says.

— Did you, you know? 8-Ball.

— It was that time of the month, Pete says.

— She's got a mouth, hasn't she?

— I had a girl once, Bugs says. The family moved away. We were close.

— How close? asks 8-Ball.

— We shared our gum.

A whistle signalling a shift change at the plant blows across town. Each of them sees the steel door sliding open, but no one enters, no one exits. The only car in the parking lot belongs to the security guard.

— Where exactly are we going? asks 8-Ball.

— Wherever we want, says Pete. He hucks a gob into the fire. Where do you want to go?

— I've never been anywhere.

— Here is somewhere, Bugs says.

— That's why we're going, isn't it? 8-Ball asks. To be someplace else?

Each sketches a picture of it in his mind. Them, there: Someplace Else.

— I hear Paris is nice, Bugs says.

— Never heard of it, says 8-Ball.

— Paris? You know: the Eiffel Tower, cheese, *romance*.

— Do you know how to get there? 8-Ball asks.

— Take the King Edward bus, Bugs says. Transfer at Cambie.

— Wrong, says Pete. You wanna go to Paris, you transfer at Commercial Drive.

Blasts from the train whistle, red lights flashing, the earth trembling.

— It's time, Pete says.

They file outside, lean into the slanting rain. 8-Ball struggles with the suitcase. They cross the road and follow a trail into the woods.

— This place we're going, does it have a beach? 8-Ball asks. Are there a lot of chicks?

— You'll have to beat them off, Pete says.

— Even me?

Iron wheels screech and kick up sparks. Soon the beast is upon them, all clang and clatter and groan, a vortex of dust and heat and fumes.

— When's it going to slow down? Bugs asks.

— It has, says Pete.

They clamber up onto the rocky rail bed. Pete sprints to an open car and tosses his shopping bags inside. He hoists himself aboard.

— Nothing to it! he hollers.

But 8-Ball's suitcase splits open; some of his clothes spill onto the tracks. Bugs retreats to lend a hand, or so he will maintain. The train disappears around the bend.

— Damn.

— Yeah.

They return to the schoolyard.

— Maybe he'll send a postcard, Bugs says.

— From Someplace Else.

Bugs takes the suitcase and hands 8-Ball the gym bag.

— Next time I'll eat first, 8-Ball says. Fries with gravy.

— With a slice of cherry pie and a cream soda chaser, says Bugs.

— Wait up!

It's Pete. He's limping, and he's left his shopping bags aboard the train.

— We thought . . .

— It started to speed up, Pete says.

His hands and knees are scraped raw from the jump. Blood is soaking through the denim.

— When I realized you guys weren't going to make it . . .

— We will next time, says 8-Ball.

— I figured it wouldn't be much fun alone.

— We should leave in the spring, says Bugs.

— Today was a dress rehearsal, 8-Ball says.

— Count me in, says Pete.

Pete's mother switches on the porch light; the door swings open. The boys have stashed their luggage behind a hedge.

At the kitchen table, simmering like a pot of soup, sits the biker Caleb Stark.

— What the fuck?

— We were tossing a football, 8-Ball explains. Pete tripped.

They think of Stark's tattoo: the snake's poisonous fangs, its rattle.

— We have to get home, 8-Ball says.

Stark's Harley is under a tarp at the side of the house.

— Keep an eye out, Bugs whispers.

— Why?

Bugs unscrews the gas cap and unzips his fly.

— This is for Pete.

8-Ball places the motorcycle helmet between his legs. He fills it to the brim, a frothy lager.

— This is for Stark, he says.

The rain lets up. Darkness moves in like a widowed aunt. Under a streetlight, they part, Bugs and 8-Ball, a couple of hungry kids with wet feet and little hope.

Dreamers.

Lovers.

Mothas.

East Side Rules

FIND YOURSELF A SEAT IN THE BLEACHERS, shell some peanuts, turn that pasty mug to the sun. Listen for the *ping* of aluminum colliding with rawhide, the softball *whooshing* beyond the jurisdiction of an outfielder's glove, and a player known as Double Cheese chugging into third base. Make it a Sunday afternoon in July, if it helps. Insert boisterous spectators along foul lines.

Of that sweltering summer afternoon, some will say Double Cheese had a large lead at third and that catcher Tubby Tuchman tried picking him off. Others maintain there was legerdemain at work, that the catcher tossed a *second* ball to his third baseman, which sailed into the outfield, encouraging the runner to trot home with the winning run.

This, though, is undisputed: before Double Cheese could cross the plate, Tubby Tuchman slapped the runner's thigh, reaching into the soft flesh of his catcher's mitt and exhibiting the game ball for all to see.

"The runner is out!" declared the umpire. "And this game is over!"

There are no stalemates in baseball. Whether it's a hard-fought nine innings or a friendly pickup affair, when the duel is done there's a winner and a loser — the reason, when a satisfactory labour contract proved elusive, Morton Hollingsworth, the "M" in M&B Landscape Supplies, agreed to consider settling the month-old dispute with seven innings of slow-pitch.

"Isn't this a little unusual?" said Dexter Beesley, the firm's UK-born accountant, when informed of the proposal. "I've never heard of wage settlements being decided by the number of . . . goals scored."

"It's baseball, Dex." Chip Hollingsworth was the proprietor's son, The Brat to employees. "In baseball, you score *runs*."

The management team was sequestered in a dusty storage bin furnished with a foldout table, the required number of uncomfortable stools, and one well-worn La-Z-Boy armchair for the boss, who suffered from backside carbuncles.

"But they have Jimmy Witherspoon," moaned Lyle Trafford, the general manager. "Didn't he play pro ball?"

"A season or two in the minors," said The Brat. "The *low* minors. Besides, he's got a gimpy back. Right, Dad? "

"Enough!" The CEO rose gingerly from the La-Z-Boy. "Our suppliers are grumbling, our competitors are gaining ground. And last night the house was egged again. Minnie's furious."

According to official company spin, all was swell.

"We're prepared to wait as long as it takes to reach a fair settlement," Hollingsworth, only the previous day, had told a reporter with the *East Side Echo*. "Our subsidiaries are having a banner year."

Which was, everyone even remotely familiar with the company knew, a mile-high pyramid of cow shit. M&B didn't have any subsidiaries, and there hadn't been anything but a cessation of revenues ever since employees, vexed by another year without a pay raise, downed tools (so to speak) and began reporting instead to strike leader Anton Malakoff. The M&B forklift driver had been living in a weathered Winnebago since his wife, tired of the rants, had given him the heave-ho.

At noon, fresh from his *tête-à-tête* with the company president, Malakoff waved his colleagues into the motorhome. Fast food wrappings and bottle caps crunched underfoot. Hand-scrubbed underthings swung from a shoelace clothesline stretched across the rear window. Empty egg cartons were stacked in a corner.

"Our side wins," Malakoff told them, "we get the raise. Lose, we return to work Monday morning, no griping."

"Seven innings?" echoed Wilf Harrelson, a part-timer. "No griping?"

"You guys wanted it settled ASAP," the strike leader reminded. In his youth Malakoff had fancied himself a Marxist.

"Actually," corrected Arnie Wick, the Afro-haired janitor and pot dealer, "our wives wanted it settled ASAP."

"Why not two games out of three?" asked Bob LeMaster, who drove the delivery truck. "Some of their guys can really hit!"

"It's our only chance for a raise," said Connie Sugar. On account of her rack, a paragon of surgical excellence, Connie managed the showroom. Some of the fellas suspected the comely single mom visited the Winnebago after hours.

"I second that," said Jimmy Witherspoon, the erstwhile pro. "We know the company's making a good profit. What have we got to lose?"

"Our jobs?" offered Hymie Toomer. Due to his years, Hymie had agreed to act as a kind of ceremonial coach and cheerleader at the proposed game. His eyes were failing. Co-workers suspected his mind was as well.

"Yeah, we've got Jimmy," Bob LeMaster said, "but he's just one of nine. Those arseholes in sales jog and go to fitness centres. A lot of our guys" — he glanced at Arnie, who was rolling a fat communal spliff — "are hallucinating most of the time."

A lineup was pencilled in on the back of an empty pizza box. Even factoring in the arseholes who jogged and attended fitness centres, most strikers figured they had a fighting chance. Many had played the game as kids and a few still tossed the ball around with their own after work. Tubby Tuchman had some pop in his bat and Andrea Sanchez, the cashier, could hit better than many of the guys. Some believed Jimmy Witherspoon, bad back or not, was the best damn ballplayer ever to come out of the East Side.

The strikers also had Buddy Paul, shipping and receiving. Buddy kept a set of free weights in his van. The walls of the vehicle were insulated with photos of

Mr. Olympus and Mr. Universe, which accounted for Buddy's nickname: *Mrs.* Paul. Though he lacked the skills required to catch a ball, everyone remembered the round tripper he smacked at the last company barbecue. Even Jimmy Witherspoon couldn't hit the ball that far.

"You in?" Malakoff asked him.

The young bodybuilder flexed his salon-bronzed pecs: affirmative.

"Okay," said the strike leader. "Let's see a show of hands."

"Hold on a sec," said Bob LeMaster. "Aren't we supposed to mark a ballot or something?"

"You, Bob," said Malakoff, "have been watching too much CBC."

"You seem very confident," LeMaster said. "This is because?"

"Because," said Malakoff, "this is the East Side. We'll be playing by East Side rules."

In the storage bin, meanwhile, management was holding its vote.

"Let's get this over with," said the company president. "I have to be on the golf course in an hour. Another one of Minnie's goddamned charity things."

Three of M&B's six managers were wary of settling the dispute with a do-or-die contest none of them were particularly good at.

"Did you see how far Buddy hit that ball?" asked Lyle Trafford. "I heard he was . . . "

Someone snickered. "Does he pitch or catch?"

"I think we should negotiate a modest raise," said Beesley. "After all, we did have another good year."

But young Hollingsworth was eager for a game.

"We can get some help," The Brat said. "I know a couple of guys. Double Cheese is every bit as good as Witherspoon."

"But he doesn't work here, Chip," protested Trafford.

"Dad and I have been talking about hiring a few sales trainees."

"You mean we're bringing in ringers?" asked Trafford. "Athletes we hire just before the game and then fire?"

"Quit worrying, we'll win," assured The Brat.

"What makes you so sure?"

"Because," said Chip, sliding shut the window and lowering his voice, "while we might be in the East Side, most of management lives on the West Side. We'll be playing by West Side rules."

Morton Hollingsworth, his backside pustules erupting, cast the tiebreaking vote.

"Okay," he decreed. "A game it is. But may God help you if we lose."

The Brat reached Malakoff on the strike leader's cell.

"Five minutes, the parking lot," he said.

Face to face with Malakoff, young Hollingsworth said, "I don't know what the old man sees in you, Anton. It's not like you're the only forklift driver in town."

"I'm not," Malakoff said. "But I am the best."

As the management team looked on from the loading ramp, and as the strikers observed from the Winnebago,

Malakoff attached his John Hancock to the agreement. Hollingsworth the Younger did likewise on behalf of M&B.

"Pay peanuts," the strike leader said, "you get monkeys."

"We've always offered competitive wages," replied The Brat. "Anywhere else, with your politics, you wouldn't be working."

"You're hardly an authority on labour, Junior," said Malakoff. "You wouldn't know a real job if it fell on you."

The deal inked — and because the *Echo* photographer had been summoned — the pair shook hands.

"The world's full of your kind," Malakoff said, grinning for the camera. "You wake up on third base and think you hit a triple."

A city-owned rectangle of mostly weeds, a shallow lake when it rained, sat adjacent to M&B's asphalt parking lot. Alongside it was a section of rusted iron bleacher, the wooden planks sprinkled with pigeon shit.

Just beyond left field bloomed a vegetable plot. It was owned by the Hongs, who were from Vietnam. Family members tended the crops under lampshade hats. Every summer the Hongs would peddle their yield to homes and businesses in the area. Many M&B employees were customers.

The most popular item was the potato — Hong potatoes, they were called, implying a kind of gold standard for taters. They were a light brown, thin-skinned delicacy responsible for the popular French fries served in the company confectionery. Each Hong spud was the size of a softball. Even the company president took home a few sacks.

"At my age," Morton Hollingsworth was fond of saying, "it's important to maintain fecal bulk."

As forecast, game day featured a glaring sun and a mild breeze — perfect for a seven-inning contest. Morton Hollingsworth was hoisted into the bed of a pickup from where he delivered a brief speech about everybody getting along. It was not lost on the strikers that he was as familiar with the subject of social harmony as his boy was with independently secured employment.

"This dispute will be settled by dinnertime today," he said. "Then we'll be family once more."

Predictably, management sycophants and their supporters applauded. Predictably, strikers and theirs didn't.

Team captains Chip Hollingsworth and Anton Malakoff, the starting chuckers, convened at home plate.

"Your lineup cards, please, gentlemen," said the umpire, a broad-beamed sort on loan from a local rec league. "Have you decided on team names?"

Little did Chip Hollingsworth know when hiring the ump — slipping him an envelope fat with appreciation — that the official was also the nephew of employee Hymie Toomer.

"We're the Reds," said the strike leader.

"That's for sure," said The Brat, squeezed into a polyester uniform, his surname and the numeral 1 newly stitched between his shoulder blades. "We'll be the Whites."

"An imaginative choice," said Malakoff.

A loonie was tossed; the Reds would bat first.

"Play ball!" hollered the ump. "And for Christ's sake, play fair."

By the fifth inning both teams had scored ten runs and several of the strikers were drunk. Just about all of them were high. Jimmy Witherspoon's bat — plus a towering three-run blast by Buddy Paul — accounted for most of the Reds' markers. The recently recruited sales trainees did the same for the Whites.

By mid-afternoon tempers on both sides were frayed as a dishrag; insults began to fly.

"Hey, you!" shouted a red-eyed Arnie Wick, referring to one of the ringers. "You must work the graveyard shift. I didn't get your name."

At M&B Landscape Supplies, there was no graveyard shift.

At the top of the sixth inning The Brat strutted to the plate. Malakoff's first pitch was a ball.

"Good eye!" screamed his father, who'd had the La-Z-Boy carted to a canvas tent behind the company's bench where he and Minnie, loyally attired in matching summer whites, sipped martinis.

The Brat slapped the next pitch into shallow centre, where it trickled like a mountain stream through Mrs. Paul's waxed gams. It turned out to be a sloppy, error-filled inning for the strikers. They entered their half of the inning down by a run.

The first Reds batter, Andrea Sanchez, was quickly retired. But then Connie Sugar dropped a blooper over the second baseman's head, putting the tying run on first. Players on both teams quietly admired the snug fit of her crimson jersey.

A murmur of anticipation rippled through the crowd as Jimmy Witherspoon completed his practice swings. The Whites called a timeout. Infielders huddled on the mound.

"Walk the big ape," advised one of the hired guns. "The spaz on deck" — Arnie — "hits like a blind man."

But the company scion balked at the idea of handing Witherspoon a free pass to pitch to a pothead. A Hollingsworth didn't give anything away for free.

"Let's hurry things up," the umpire said. "It'll be Christmas soon."

The Brat opted to challenge Witherspoon — or at least appear to. The first two offerings were wide of the plate. Ball three almost cleared the backstop. A chorus of boos rained down on the M&B heir.

"Chickenshit!"

The fourth toss was high and outside, but Witherspoon leaned out over the plate and tomahawked the ball into right-centre. It soared over Dexter Beesley's confused head, nestling amongst a patch of dandelions. The Reds' cleanup hitter lazily circled the bases.

That same inning, the bases empty, Buddy Paul hit his second round-tripper. This one went even farther than the first.

The Reds were up two runs going into the bottom half of the final frame.

Malakoff's arthritic arm was beginning to ache. He fanned the first batter but walked the second, who advanced a base on a passed ball. Andrea Sanchez in left field then switched places with Malakoff. She promptly induced Dexter Beesley, whose bat couldn't recognize a ball, to whiff for the fourth time.

Double Cheese, the next batter, tapped some dirt from his cleats and freed his sweat-drenched underpants from the crack of his beef-fed rump.

"Problem?" shouted Arnie. "Got letters in the mailbox, do ya?"

The Whites' ringer answered with a high drive to left-centre, splitting the outfielders. A more fleet-footed batsman would have made a four-bagger out of it, tying the game, but Double Cheese pulled up winded at third. He'd had his customary two cheeseburgers and several Heinekens for lunch.

What happened next depends on whom one talks to, on where one was positioned, and perhaps on how much drugs and alcohol one had consumed. Did Double Cheese dash for home, as the Reds maintained? Or did Tubby Tuchman intentionally overthrow a second, illegitimate ball to entice the runner, as the Whites believed?

The ump claims he was momentarily rendered sightless in the late afternoon glare. By the time he'd regained his vision, Double Cheese was charging down the line, and catcher Tubby Tuchman was tagging him with the game ball.

Final score: Reds 16, Whites 15.

Half the spectators were outraged, half ebullient. Several Whites threatened the ump, who had to be escorted to his car. And while work did resume the following morning, as per the accord, the post-game picnic was cancelled. Later that night the strikers had themselves a victory bash in the Winnebago. Connie Sugar stayed over.

Years have passed. The Brat has inherited the company, the La-Z-Boy, and the debilitating Hollingsworth abscesses. There's still a picnic every year, but it's a poorly attended affair, and there are no more softball matches. Anton Malakoff found work as a union rep with the steel-workers, denying M&B's new chief executive officer the satisfaction of sacking him. And yes, employees did get their raise, but it was a token sum, and there hasn't been another since. As punishment for their losing perfor-mance, the Whites received a salary rollback.

Obsessed with rehashing the contested game, Chip Hollingsworth continues to claim the Reds cheated that day. He insists the catcher did make a throw to third, just as the ump was temporarily decommissioned, and that it was intentionally errant. Tubby Tuchman, The Brat says, must have been concealing the game ball under his chest protector, waiting for just such an opportunity.

The Reds argued that if this theory was true, that another ball had been put into play as a ruse to deceive the runner, verification would have been found in the vegetable plot, where the alleged second ball came to rest. With the bewildered Hong clan looking on, The Brat had commanded teammates to drop to their grass-stained knees and overturn every leaf in the garden. A second ball was never retrieved.

Alice Bird

AFTER DOTTIE'S DEATH, A RESPECTABLE mourning period having passed, I signed up for a creative writing class at the seniors' centre. Whenever riled I'd always fired off a letter to the newspaper or to a retailer who'd provided poor service. Was I was capable of writing something substantial? A short story maybe, or even a book?

Our instructor, Leanne Davidson, had published a few poems in an online literary journal. None rhymed, and most featured Leanne underneath or on top of a "partner" other than a lawful spouse — free verse about free sex.

My fellow students didn't seem to mind. They welcomed her that first night with vegetarian snacks and herbal teas. Before dismissing us Leanne recommended we each produce a writing sample for our next meeting. It could be on any subject at all.

"Writers," she said, "this is your chance to say what's been on your minds."

From her poetry I knew what was often on Leanne's. In the parking lot afterwards I told her what was on mine.

"I look forward to reading it, writer," she said. "Everyone enjoys a murder mystery."

"Emmett," I said. "Emmett McNish."

"The birds didn't live in trees," my story began, "they lived next door." Hamish Bird was a postman. His wife Louise suffered from a nervous condition, which is how polite folks in those days referred to someone who was crazy. Alice was the couple's only child. When Louise required hospital care, and because Dottie had always pined for kids, we cared for the girl. There would be a shy knock at the door, and we'd know Louise had gone off her rocker again.

Alice lived with us for however long it took doctors to stabilize Louise. The girl needed us, and we her. We couldn't have been more pleased had we ordered a child from a catalogue. Dottie and I even talked about adopting Alice, about putting her in our will. After a bath she smelled like a freshly halved mango.

Dottie taught Alice how to cook. I was a bookkeeper, so I became her math tutor. But Alice wasn't interested in recipes or numbers. She wanted to take one of those modelling courses advertised in teen magazines. She believed it would lead to a glamorous film career.

"I want to begin with small parts," she said.

"You don't want to be a star?" I teased. "Isn't that the whole idea?"

"Not right away," she said. "I want to work up to that."

I assured Alice something could be arranged: small roles to start, international adulation to follow.

What remained of Louise eventually managed to stay clear of the hospital, and Alice left us. Soon after Dottie began feeling poorly. I took early retirement to care for her. And Alice? She changed. By the time she was in high school her visits had slowed to infrequent. That progressed to her pretending not to notice us when we were puttering in the garden. It was as if the girl we knew had been replaced by someone who skipped school and ran around with boys. Her default demeanour was a scowl.

"Alice," I wrote, "had become a stranger."

Louise, heavily medicated, didn't seem to notice; her "baby girl" could do no wrong. Hamish probably did, but he was uncomfortable with words and said nothing. But there was plenty to notice. Alice wore short skirts that in our day would have gotten a young lady indicted. Each time I saw her in one I was reminded of my mother's admonition to my sisters: if it's not for sale, don't put it in the window.

Leanne returned our first drafts. Comments were scribbled in the margins. "You have my interest," went one, "but you have to remember that people bore easily these days, Emmett. With social media and the TV remote, attention spans aren't what they were."

One day Hamish confided that Alice was going with Dewey Foster, a local delinquent I had always suspected of spray painting filthy language on our garage door.

Whenever we heard rock music, we knew Dewey and his transistor radio were in the vicinity. Angry guitar chords announced him. The drum solos made our windows rattle.

Dewey and Alice were inseparable. They would smooch and grope each other anywhere, anytime; it didn't seem to matter who was around. They did it in the park. They did it behind the school. They also did it on the Birds' back porch, which was visible from our kitchen window.

"They're lucky Hamish isn't seeing this," I said to Dottie, by then in a wheelchair. "The two of them are going at it again. He's sticking his tongue down her throat!"

"It's called French kissing," said Dottie, who didn't anger often. I think she held out hope the girl would return to her old self someday, and then return to us.

"There's a phrase editors are fond of," Leanne told me one night after class: "'Cut to the chase.'"

She was referring to my story. It was becoming unwieldy.

"A novel is a marriage," Leanne said. "You can take your time, let things play out. A short story is a one-night stand. That means . . . "

"I'm old," I said. "Not retarded."

One bone-chilling autumn evening, Dewey Foster plunged a kitchen knife into Alice, or so it was alleged. Louise opened the back door to let out the cat and there she was, her baby girl. I joined several concerned neigh-bours in the Birds' backyard.

"It poked up out of her chest like cutlery left in a heap of unappetizing food," I wrote. "If it wasn't for all the blood, you might think Alice was gazing up at the equinox."

The police arrived promptly, blocking off the street.

"Any clue as to who might have done this?" a detective asked Hamish.

"Her ex," he managed. "They split up a few weeks ago. Alice worked at a travel agency; I think she was sweet on someone there. Dewey was crazy jealous."

One week after he was picked up, the boy was charged with murder and held without bail. He'd only recently turned nineteen. In those days, in our neck of the woods, that made Dewey an adult.

Everyone figured Dewey would confess, as it was rumoured Alice's blood was found on his person. But then his legal aid lawyer, Ray Townsend, announced his client would be pleading not guilty. Dottie was bedridden by the time the trial started. A friend offered to look in on her while I testified. I stayed on for the proceedings. I'd seen plenty of murder trials on TV. I'd always wanted to see the real thing.

"You'd be surprised how many people were lining up for a seat," I told Dottie, although I doubt she understood Alice was gone. "It was like they were queuing for a movie. A man was eating popcorn."

Neighbours accustomed to Dewey Foster swaggering along our streets in his leather jacket and tight jeans wouldn't have recognized him in the courtroom, not with that white shirt and clip-on tie. His rat's nest of a hairdo was shorn, too — on lawyer Townsend's instructions, I'll bet. Dewey the choirboy.

I testified that, in the months prior to the murder, I'd often noticed someone dropping Alice off late at night. I saw a profile in the glow of the dashboard lights and heard a voice, a man's.

"Was it the defendant?" Dewey's lawyer asked me.

"Dewey, drive? He couldn't balance a bicycle."

The prosecutor, David Poole, quizzed a policeman about visiting the defendant's home the evening of the murder. Mrs. Foster said the boy had been out all day. The premises were searched.

"Was there any sign of him?" Poole asked.

"Our guys saw a young fella in the alley who fit his description," the constable said. "But he took off."

"The defendant fled?"

"Somebody did."

On cross, Townsend asked the policeman, "Isn't it true Dewey had several outstanding warrants the night you visited the Foster residence?"

"He was suspected of cruelty to animals and possession of a controlled substance," the officer confirmed.

"Is it possible he was trying to avoid being picked up on those charges?" Townsend probed. "That he didn't know what had happened to Alice?"

"Anything's possible."

A second policeman told of visiting the home of Alice's travel agency boss, Peter Dalrymple. It had been established that he was the man I'd seen dropping her off.

"Mrs. Dalrymple said her husband was sleeping," the officer said.

"Did you wake him?" asked the prosecutor.

"We apprehended him climbing out a rear window."

After the lunch break Dalrymple was asked by the Crown why he didn't exit his home via the door.

"I had to tell the wife about me and Alice before she read it in the papers," he said.

"How thoughtful," Poole said. "But why the window?"

"She was rummaging around in the closet."

"And that is germane to this court because . . . "

"The Mrs. plays softball. She keeps her bat in the closet."

The prosecution also quizzed Mr. Altonin, who lived next door to the Fosters, about seeing Dewey in the alley the night of the murder.

"I was taking out the trash," he said. "Dewey and the girl often smoked pot behind my garage."

"Did you notice anything unusual about him?" Poole pressed.

"Everything about Dewey is unusual," Mr. Altonin said. "But that night there was something sticky on the bottom of his sneakers."

"Tell the court what happened the following day."

"I noticed a footprint in the alley. When the police came around asking questions, they took a look. It was blood."

Poole held up a pair of Dewey's sneakers; they had been marked Exhibit B. An expert testified that the blood found on the soles of both was O Positive, the same as Alice's. (We didn't know about DNA back then.) Exhibit A was the rusty kitchen knife removed from Alice. Its wooden handle had been wiped clean of fingerprints.

Defence lawyer Townsend must have concluded the jury wasn't buying his version of events, because he elected to have Dewey take the stand — a risky strategy, I'd heard. Defendants are usually advised to shut their pie holes and let the Crown prove its case.

There was a collective gasp in the courtroom when Dewey took the oath. All eyes seemed fixed on the right hand resting atop the New Testament — many, no doubt, picturing it slamming Exhibit A into Alice.

When it was his turn to question Dewey, Poole requested a brief recess. An assistant hurried from the courtroom, returning moments later with a rectangular cardboard box. Of course Poole could have arrived with the box, but it was so much more dramatic halting the proceedings and having a subaltern waltz back in bearing evidence critical to the case. Besides, it left the defendant squirming on the witness stand, the eyes of the disapproving upon him.

The prosecutor asked Dewey to show the jury the contents of the box; it was a turtleneck sweater.

"Alice gave it to me for my birthday," he said.

"Why was your sweater in Alice's bedroom?"

"I returned it after she dumped me. I stuffed it back in the box and left it at her door."

Prosecutor Poole turned to the jury.

"Is that why you stabbed her to death? Because she dumped you?"

Dewey responded with language I will not repeat here. Poole then asked if there was anything else in the box. There was: a note. It was sealed inside a plastic evidence bag.

"Could you read it to the court?"

Dewey studied the slip of paper.

"I can't remember what I wrote, but it wasn't this," he said.

Counsel for both sides conferred with the judge, who asked the court stenographer to read the note.

"You said we'd be together till the end of time," she read aloud. "You two-timing bitch, I'll get you for this."

"Is the note signed?" Poole asked her.

"The note is typed," she said. "So is the signature — Dewey."

Exhibit C.

I knew from watching my crime procedurals that a trial is nearing its conclusion when the character witnesses are called. Besides his mother, Dewey had only one, a church minister who said the boy was "misunderstood," that his bad attitude was "harmless teenage posturing."

"How many times, and for how long on each occasion did you meet with the defendant?" prosecutor Poole asked the clergyman.

"I didn't actually *meet* with him," the minister, reddening, admitted.

"But you told police . . . "

"We talked on the phone."

"For how long? Remember, we can subpoena those records."

The minister dabbed his forehead with a handkerchief.

"For at least five minutes."

It took the jury two hours to find Dewey guilty of first degree murder. It took the judge even less to decide his fate. Because the note proved intent, Dewey received a life sentence with no parole possible until he'd served twenty-five years.

A newspaper columnist attending the trial speculated that it likely took "all of two minutes" to reach the verdict, suggesting jurors might well have passed the time "playing a round of Hearts." He concluded, "There was nothing to debate, no evidence to weigh. Dewey Foster is a cold-blooded killer. That's what was good about the good old days. Back then, this punk would swing without further ado."

Leanne returned our stories at the last class. "Nice work," she wrote at the top of mine. We had a little party for her, everything organic. I was hoping she'd elaborate in the parking lot.

"I think you've got something here," is all she said. "Don't be afraid to revise. The best do, endlessly. They say a story is never really finished, only abandoned."

The story about Alice would be my first and only attempt. If nothing else, the class at the seniors' centre had taught me that Emmett McNish was meant to keep books, not write them. I told Leanne that if I reconsidered, I'd send her a draft.

She handed me her card. "Do," she said. "Maybe we can find a publisher."

If I'd been writing a confession and not fiction, I might have mentioned the night I went next door to the Birds to return a bottle of Windex. I found the sweater box Dewey had left at the door; the writing on the outside was familiar to me. It was the same hand that had defiled my garage door.

I took the box back to my house. The letter inside bristled with anger and heartbreak, but Dewey had not threatened revenge. I chewed on things a spell before replacing the letter with one composed on my old Smith Corona typewriter. I inserted Dewey's name at the bottom and returned it to the Birds' back door before anyone was the wiser. Police found it in Alice's room the night of the murder, still unopened. As to how her blood made its way to Dewey's sneakers, I can only guess he testified truthfully — that he came by the house after the deed was done. He assumed he'd be blamed and ran off, but not before sloshing around in it.

There wasn't anything said during the trial about the validity of the note or the significance of the typewriter;

we didn't have computers in those days. Still, I was expecting forensic experts to investigate, the reason I tossed my Smith Corona into a farmer's slough. I thought Townsend would put up more of a fight, anything to muddy the waters, like they do on TV, but he just seemed to run out of steam.

If you suspect I'm a dirty old man who molested Alice as a child and was trying to cover it up, you'd be wrong. I'm not that sort. You see, the girl we once thought of as our own had dropped us long before she dropped Dewey. Anger fades in some; it compounds in others.

As the end neared Dottie didn't have the strength to gum food. Just before slipping away she opened her eyes, a last glimpse of the world that had disappointed her so.

"Alice . . . " My Dottie never uttered another word.

Dewey took Alice from us. I think it was the pot and the rock music. It was the French kissing, her age, the times — a confluence of circumstances. To us — to me — Alice had died long before that frigid night on the back porch. How happy the three of us could have been.

All things considered, though, I'd say the books have been balanced. By the time Dewey is released from prison, I'll be gone. The lawyer handling my affairs was instructed to get this draft to Leanne after I'd passed.

If you're reading this, I have.

The Robin's Egg

HENRY FOUND STANTON, THE MAN HE'D TALKED to on the phone, where he said he would be: concealed beneath a Canucks cap, in a pub called Your Father's Moustache. The waiter plopped down two Heinekens and Stanton plopped down two vials, one slightly larger than the other.

"A few drops from the small vial will make you drowsy," he said. "When you are, drain the taller one right away. It kicks in after you've fallen asleep. You won't feel a thing."

"Like I told you on the phone," Henry said, "it's for a friend."

"Of course it is." Stanton took a sip of beer. "I should go. Others are waiting."

Corrine knew Henry would receive the test results on Monday. Neither mentioned the fact in the days prior or slept much the night before, although in that drizzly dawn both claimed to have done so soundly.

Henry expected Corrine to call on her break, but he needed time to think through what he had to say, so he disembarked from the train two stops early and walked the remaining soggy kilometres. The message light was flashing on the house phone inside the rear door. Before his shoes were unlaced, it rang again. Henry knew Corrine was responsible for the impatient ring, and she knew he was incapable of ignoring one.

"Was I right?" she asked. "A benign cyst?"

"You have cancer, I'm afraid," said Dr. Arlene Lehman, "and it's metastasized. But we have a few procedures that might buy you some time."

"I'm going to die?"

"We're all going to die, Mr. North," she said. "Some of us catch the early show."

Disease. Metastasize. Henry was having difficulty absorbing it all. Twenty minutes earlier he'd been sipping a decaf at Starbucks. At the initial visit a miniature camera had been inserted into his nostril and down his throat. Dr. Lehman found nothing amiss. A biopsy did.

To Henry, bad news had always meant things like earthquakes and home invasions and pileups on the freeway. The list would now also include what he had contracted: squamous cell carcinoma. It began in the throat as a dry cough and spread like peanut butter to lymph nodes in his neck.

Dr. Lehman dimmed the lights and flipped a switch; his scan flashed on the monitor. There was the skull, a row of teeth. The largest tumour sat alongside his Adam's apple. It looked as though he had swallowed a robin's egg.

"Henry?"

Corrine worked for a clothing retailer. In the background he could hear sales clerks chatting up customers, the cash drawer slamming shut. He'd been cool as an ocean breeze when the doctor delivered her findings. Now, despite several attempts, the words he needed to convey wouldn't form in his blighted throat.

"I'm coming home," she said.

Henry stretched out on the bed where years earlier he'd implanted into an ovulating Corrine the seedlings that would sprout into Jake, a high school physics teacher, and Allison, an accountant like her father. Corrine's Mazda was soon gliding into the carport, the railing shaking as she bounded across the porch. When it was done, his words liberated, her sobs echoed through the house. Henry, who hadn't had a good howl since almost crushing his nuts in a bicycle accident as a child, joined her, an alien mewl erupting from his lungs.

"Oh, Henry," Corrine sighed.

For the first few days we were in shock, Henry emailed William, a friend living in the UK. *But now — and this might seem crazy — we're going at it like monkeys. It's like we're nineteen again.*

Or maybe it's me saying, "There's been a mistake! Can a sick man do this?"

It began in, of all places, the laundry room, culminating atop a heap of soiled sheets and crusty socks, a whiff of detergent in the musty basement air.

Some people, when they're ill, revel in the attention. Not Henry North. At the mining firm where he worked each expression of sympathy proved awkward. He wished he hadn't blabbed, but it couldn't be helped: a replacement had to be recruited.

Henry realized he'd once looked upon those who'd been similarly cursed the same way colleagues, with their tight smiles and lowered eyes, now regarded him. Hugs, backslaps . . . he felt stained. He wasn't in flight just yet, jetting off to the great hereafter, but he did sense he was in the departure lounge of his life, quaffing a final brew.

Several co-workers used the phrase, "If you need anything, don't hesitate to ask." Henry thought of talking to Peter Sharpe in marketing, who was one of them, about patching the roof. Dennis Collins, the vice-president, also expressed a willingness to assist. Over the winter raccoons had moved into the garden shed; Henry was afraid to open the door. Wasn't Dennis always boasting about his hunting prowess?

"My cousin felt under the weather one morning," said Carol Tyler, an administrative assistant, slipping into Henry's office. "He was dead by dinner."

Cataloguing the misfortunes of others, he understood, was how some people handled such news. They don't know what else to say. He'd done it himself.

"I'll be sure to have a good lunch, Carol," he said.

Eve Westingham from personnel told him her first husband had also discovered a lump.

"Gord's was under his arm," she said. "They gave him six months. He survived four years, so what do doctors know?"

"I remember Gord from the Christmas banquet," Henry said. "He seemed like a swell guy."

"Actually," Eve corrected, "he was an asshole."

Each time a well-wisher requested a private moment Henry felt obligated to share something. So he'd undo a button and loosen his tie.

"Touch it," he said of the robin's egg. "Go ahead: it doesn't hurt."

Most, squeamish, declined.

After centuries of war and plague, Henry emailed William, *you'd think humans would have developed a protocol for dealing with death; at the very least a manual, an app. When you really need them, words are as useless as paper bags in the rain.*

Though they talked on the phone and exchanged dispatches regularly, Henry and Corrine hadn't seen William and Millie in years. Henry had other friends in town, and good ones, too, but none like his old amigo, who still hadn't responded to his most recent overture. But then Corrine reminded him the couple had mentioned something about a cruise.

"What was it William said about cruising?" Henry asked.

"That it was like imprisonment," Corrine recalled, "with a chance of drowning."

Officially decommissioned, Henry found himself with plenty of spare time on his hands. He hadn't a clue what to do with it. Everything had happened so quickly. One day he had a fine head of hair, the next, the first blast of toxins having made their way along his bloodstream, the locks were clogging the shower drain. The doctors, his employer, Corrine, and the kids all urged him to take it easy. But Henry knew how to take it easy about as well as he knew how to ride a unicycle.

It being spring, he began to mow the grass. Wednesdays he mowed vertically, Saturdays, horizontally. It was something he'd seen on the Home and Garden TV network. He trimmed the borders with a new gas-fuelled edger from Black & Decker. He might not be able to control his disease, but he was damn well going to govern his lawn.

In the park where he fed kitchen scraps to the ducks, he became acquainted with a population he hadn't known existed, people who, like himself, passed afternoons wandering the trails and warming its benches, parsing the sentiments expressed on the memorial plaques. Since it was midday, he supposed most park visitors were unemployed or retired. A few, he suspected, were unbalanced or on the lam. He knew he wasn't the only one waiting to die.

"See ya, then," he would say after chatting up old Fred, who'd fought in the Korean War and had a wonky ticker.

"Hope so," Fred would reply, shuffling off.

Henry was happiest on the backyard deck with his *Field Guide to Birds* and powerful binoculars. Most of the avian action occurred next door, in Mel and Dotty Sprackmans' cottonwood. He jotted down all sightings in a log, recording the numbers, weather conditions and arrival time of darting chickadees and red-shafted flickers, of every purple finch and dark-eyed junco. He noted as well the daily presence of a sabre-beaked pigeon hawk on the telephone wire at the end of the alley, predator to all of the above.

His slumping spirits rallied when William's name popped up on the computer screen.

My name is Lynn, William's daughter, the message began. *My mother tells me you once worked with my dad, and that we met when I was a child. I'm sorry to tell you that he passed away while on a Mediterranean cruise. It was the smoking.*

Henry took the news hard. He and Corrine commiserated with Millie on the phone.

"If there's anything I can do," Henry heard himself say, "anything at all . . . "

A dog was loitering outside the rear gate. It appeared lame or lost. Henry had Munchy Mart deliver an assortment of dog chow.

"It seems confused," said Corrine.

"Who isn't?" Henry said.

Corrine snapped a photo of the animal, a male, and emailed it to the SPCA.

"I think he's blind in one eye," she said. "And what dog doesn't bark?"

"The dog that only moments ago peed on your carpet."

When the SPCA told them it hadn't received any inquiries, the Norths decided to adopt. They named the dog Zero.

After the second round of chemo, the nausea beginning to recede, Henry took advantage of a special offer for delivery of the local newspaper. Like many people his age, despite the regrettable loss of trees, he preferred the tactile to the virtual — newsprint in his hands, ink on the fingers. No online news sites for him. He'd always picked up the weekend edition for the TV highlights and sports scores, but he'd never studied current affairs. World events to him were whatever was in the headlines. He wasn't sure why, but he wanted to learn more about the planet he might soon depart.

Early the following morning he heard a *thwack* at the door and there it was, wrapped in a plastic bag. He promptly retreated to the deck and read the paper front to back. He devoured minutia about the battle in Benghazi. Same with the tsunami in Japan. All those people swept away like soapsuds.

In the obituaries there was occasionally a face he recognized: someone from the clinic, a former neighbour or teacher, a long-forgotten playmate. The section was overpopulated by men portrayed as strong and selfless and women eulogized for tidy homes and artery-clogging pastries. If everyone who'd croaked had been so saintly, he mused, who caused all the misery on earth?

"And who," he asked Zero — since William's passing, Henry's new confidante — "molested all those kids?"

Corrine was the family's fount of encouragement. She would insist the disease was something one fought; Henry considered it something you avoided, and if you couldn't, something to endure. She believed in banishing negativity from every conversation, he in playing out your hand, being a good sport until the end. He had never been fond of Disney endings, and he didn't believe in miracles. His had been a good life. If there was such a thing, he hoped for a good death.

Henry began to suspect Corrine wasn't doing as well as she let on. He'd been mowing the lawn and had come inside for a glass of water. He could hear her weeping in the spare room. Over the following few days she developed a rash. The creases in her face multiplied.

Corrine's friend Adele told them about several remedies she believed could do for Henry what his doctors couldn't. Her business card read: Spiritual Advisor. Dream lofty dreams, and as you dream, so shall you become.

"Not interested," Henry said.

"I don't know why," Corrine objected. "It doesn't hurt to try them."

But Corrine did know why. In the thirty-five years the Norths had been married, they'd had the same conversation many times.

"Her potions haven't been tested," Henry reiterated. "Any evidence of health benefits is anecdotal. We also don't know how they might interact with my medications."

Adele was forever going off on retreats featuring assorted swamis or faith healers. She'd paid a substantial sum to walk barefoot across hot coals. She appeared never to have encountered an unsubstantiated idea she couldn't support. We're surrounded by extraterrestrials! The government is reading our emails! The latter turned out to be true, but Henry didn't think it prudent to replace his oncologist with someone who believed dropping nail clippings into cat urine could ward off evil spirits.

Her remedies for what afflicted Henry included shark cartilage from Mexico and a tea made from fungi growing on birch trees in China. Whatever concoction Adele flogged was never something as attainable as a dandelion pushing through a local slab of sidewalk. Before it could be sold to the gullible and the desperate, a marketable elixir required an exotic locale.

Yet Henry relented. He'd drink the tea. "I'll do it for you, Corr," he said. "But don't assume I want to play for the team."

The mixture tasted just as it looked — like mud — though it did the trick: Corrine returned to her vivacious self, or so she wanted the family to believe. The rash did disappear. She began applying makeup again and added a splash of colour to her hair. Sensing a breach in his cynicism, she tried persuading Henry to try Adele's shark bone soup.

"Don't push your luck," Henry replied, "or I'll report you to the Martian police."

"I'll cast a spell on you," Corrine said. "Don't think I won't!"

"If you coulda," he said, "You woulda."

Henry wished he hadn't learned so late in life the value of a good cry. Like most men, he'd been taught to suck it up. Out on the deck one day his mind began to drift. Afterwards he couldn't remember what he'd been thinking, but his cheeks were streaked with tears, the front of his shirt moist. It got so that he could start bawling while standing in the checkout line at the drugstore. He could be changing his socks. Henry cried for days when William passed. A memory could unleash a torrent. Sometimes the melancholy was caused by an unmanly self-pity that embarrassed him, but most of the time it had something to do with Corrine and the kids. He feared most of all leaving them unprotected, prey to the pigeon hawks of the world. He suspected the medications were messing with his mind.

Would fate, he wondered, be kind to his successors? It was his greatest anxiety. He couldn't countenance the image that sometimes seeped into his thoughts — of Corrine, his ashes long since scattered, snuggling up to a pinch-hitter.

About a year after the diagnosis, the robin's egg excised, Dr. Manwearing, a palliative specialist, informed Henry that the cancer had leapfrogged to his lungs, bowel, and brain. The news didn't come as a surprise. His test results hadn't been favourable, and he could feel things weren't right. Corrine strained to remain positive.

So, too, did Dr. Manwearing. "We'll mount a vigorous defence," he said. "We haven't used up all our gunpowder."

In anticipation of the inevitable, Henry hired an elderly Japanese gardener to manicure his precious grass. Sasumo was selected from several qualified candidates because he shared Henry's appreciation of turf symmetry. He glided nimbly across the lawn, a kind of landscapers' ju-jitsu. The yard had never looked so fine.

Whereas Henry's treatments to date had been exhausting but bearable, the new treatment wasn't. Days after the inaugural drip, crossing a room was like wading through wet cement. His mouth became as dry as the Sahara. Expensively crowned and annually cleaned teeth now wobbled in his blistered gums. Radiation destroyed his taste buds; he had to force himself to eat. Henry and Corrine's amorous afternoons were reduced to holding hands.

Soon he couldn't swallow without pain, and then, waking one morning, he couldn't swallow at all. Until the swelling abated he was fed through a tube threaded into his abdomen. In a month he lost the last of his paunch.

He began to view the cancer not as an illness, but as the Devil to cast out. He lay on his back in the radiotherapy unit, white-frocked lab techs in their hermetically sealed booths bombing the marauding tumours. He imagined his caregivers as priests sprinkling his enfeebled limbs with holy water. This wasn't health care, it was an exorcism.

Corrine drove him, if he felt up to it, to group meetings at the clinic. He found it helpful to get out of the house, to commune with folks in the same leaky boat. When ill, it's always salutary to see people worse off than yourself.

One day at the clinic he fell into conversation with a familiar face.

"I'm Roy," the man said. "Melanoma. Sure glad I'm not living in the States. I couldn't afford this."

He was referring, Henry assumed, not just to the excellent care but the paintings by native artists lining the walls and the jazz on the sound system. Volunteers would soon be serving coffee and jelly donuts.

"Me neither," Henry said.

"In the US," Roy said, "you can get great medical care as long as you have the cash or some kind of insurance plan."

"I heard that, too," said Henry.

"Everyone can afford it up here . . . but you might not survive the wait."

"Eat all your greens," Henry advised.

They were joined by Earl, leukemia, a few seats over.

"I think it's grand that people are running marathons and such to raise money for research," Earl said. "Many cancers are now curable. Not mine, though. I probably won't be here this time next year."

"The way I feel," Henry said, "the next few minutes are iffy."

"Doctors can now tell many of us what we'll die of, even when," Earl said, "but there seems to be more cancer around than ever. In the old days people just got sick and died. Remember?"

"I do," Henry said.

"Me, too," said Roy.

"It was old age, people would say, and everybody seemed happy with that."

A bald woman sitting nearby — Liz, both mountainous breasts — lowered her book and said, "Who needs advance notice? Imagine being told that in two years you were going to be hit by a bus."

Roy said, "My father believed it was best to die in battle. It's quick, and sure to come with a medal."

"You can never have enough of those," Henry agreed.

"With all the medicine they have nowadays," Earl said, "people hang on for years. Me? I can't take a decent shit. If that's progress, then I'm Elvis."

"I thought you looked familiar," said Henry.

"What if they cured it, huh?" Earl asked, looking at each of them. "Think about it: where would they put us all?"

"You know why men usually die before their wives?" Roy asked.

Henry didn't. Neither did Liz. Even know-it-all Earl was stumped.

"The husbands go first," Roy said, "because they want to."

While Henry was waiting for his appointment with Dr. Manwearing, security guards chased off a man handing out a flyer. It was from a group called InCharge, and it talked about how final stage patients like Henry could end their lives painlessly.

"You should be able to decide when to pass based on your own beliefs, not on medieval religious dogma," it said. "We don't allow our pets to suffer."

The flyer advertised a website. That afternoon, Corrine at yoga, Henry made the call. A recorded message instructed him to leave a phone number.

Ever since the robin's egg, Henry had thought about ending his life. About buying a handgun and disappearing into the woods or jumping from a bridge. He'd considered locking himself in an idling car with a garden hose duct-taped to the muffler. But then he read on the Internet that carbon monoxide poisoning didn't always work because of lower emission standards. It could leave one alive, and with brain damage. Phenobarbital seemed best, but it was hard to get, and helium gas, another option, required the assistance of others. The InCharge website explained that its "solution" had been invented by unemployed chemistry grads.

Was taking your own life cowardice or courage? And could he go through with it? His replies to those questions would depend on what day he was asked, on the intensity of the fatigue, and the resilience of his spirit at any given time.

This, though, he knew: it wasn't death he feared, it was the dying. The pain. The dry-heaving. Shitting yourself and lying in it for hours. A quick passing would also save the family a load of grief. Corrine was ready to implode — the rash was back, and he knew Jake and

Allison were having a hard time. A counsellor at the clinic had told him, "When a member of your family gets cancer, you all get it."

Stanton reached Henry on his cell. They discussed the InCharge fee.

"That seems kind of pricey for a couple of vials and a how-to video," Henry said. "My friend isn't rich, and I'm guessing there aren't any pretty girls in your DVD."

"There are no tolls on most bridges, either," Stanton said.

They agreed to meet at a bar downtown, Your Father's Moustache.

"Bring cash," Stanton said.

"What, no easy payment plan?"

On the deck, almost dusk. The shadows in the garden have lengthened and there is a nip in the brittle autumn air. Earlier in the day Sasumo made the last cut of the season. A tank of oxygen sits under Henry's chair; plastic prongs are pinned to his nostrils.

"You know," he addresses Zero, "I might be dying, but I've never felt so effing alive. The moments count. Weird, huh?"

The hound responds as he often does when Henry philosophizes: by lifting an arthritic leg . . . and noisily licking its balls.

All the house lights are out and the back door is open wide when Corrine, home from work, eases the Mazda into the carport. A gust of wind sweeps into the yard, and a loose sheet of Henry's newspaper unravels, rolling itself into a ball. It skips up the flagstone walkway, coming to rest on his perfect lawn.

"Henry? Are you there?"

She runs through the kitchen and along the hallway, switching on the lights. She looks in the bathroom and down the stairwell leading to the basement.

Out on the deck, Zero rests his snout in Henry's lap. A letter addressed to Corrine and one for each of the kids are held in place by a stone from the garden. An empty vial rolls between his legs.

"Damn it, Henry! Where are you?"

When he was in treatment, his mind muddled by the chemo, he used to have this dream. It's winter. Corrine is walking home from the Munchy Mart. Her hair has turned white as a fresh dump of snow; bereavement is etched into her brow. She looks up at their house and realizes — as she does now, stepping onto the deck — that her Henry isn't anywhere anymore.

Brunch with the Jackals

I

There are three people in the canoe. Two have a pulse. The body lies under a nylon tarp, an involuntary stowaway. Bits of a bracelet clasped to the inanimate wrist collide whenever the paddlers shift position. Save for a flicker of campfire on the far shore, the only light drips from a brilliant pinch of moon. All else is shadow and reflection and supposition, and then the dark mass of those weary hills.

"Give it up," he says from the stern. "You're useless."

She pulls her paddle from the water; the canoe skims like a skate on ice.

A squat willow tree sprouts from Wigwam Rock, where sheltered channel gives way to open water. He has told her about how aboriginal legend demands boaters offer sacrifice here: a ring, an earring, a bottle of beer.

"Just drop it over the side," he says.

The reporter Harry Shapka was in a dockside coffee bar when he received the fateful call.

"Shapka? The boss asked me to fetch you."

"What's up, Archie? A decision's been made about the parking meters, I bet."

Archie Meeks, the *Rail Spur Record* copy boy. At thirty-six, an unsuccessful skirt chaser still residing in his parents' mouldy basement.

"There's been an accident. A bad one."

"Speak up! I'm at Café Casa."

"There's been a collision on Orchard Road. A golfer phoned it in."

"What's the matter," Harry asked. "Delmonico too busy powdering her nose?"

Sandi Delmonico, trainee reporter. Niece of despised publisher, Ed Leatherdale.

"She took a sick day," Archie said. "Cramps, probably."

Harry stepped outside. The air reeked of burning oil. Plumes of smoke drifted like rainclouds over Tullaine Lake.

Orchard Road proved impassable. Already present were police vehicles, Rail Spur's lone ambulance, the volunteer fire truck and an expanding congress of carnage voyeurs. Harry parked the Cherokee and grabbed his camera. He found police chief Norval Spikes considering a sports car's crumpled remains.

"Somebody said it was a Shackleford," Harry said. "Do we know which one?"

"The wrong one," the chief said. "Suzanne."

Harry had recently interviewed Suzanne Shackleford about Shoreline Lodge. When completed it would be the town's first five-star resort. A former fashion model, still very much a beauty, Suzanne had returned to Rail Spur to see the project through after Andrew Shackleford, her grandfather, had expired. She lived at the family home now — a sprawling, neglected Victorian — with a younger brother, Barry. Andrew's widow Margaret, who had helped raise the siblings, resided in the local care home.

After the interview Suzanne had had the contractor Brian Langdon show Harry around the site. They came across an Oriental youth playing a lugubrious melody on a bamboo flute.

"Kenji," Langdon said. "He belongs to Barry."

"I'll keep that in mind," Harry said.

Shards of windshield littered the accident scene. Harry winced at the thought of what must have happened to the face that once graced the catwalks of Milan and Paris.

"The truck was towing a trailer," Norval said. He dropped to one knee, examining the skid marks. "The driver said he swung into a turn just as she was cresting the hill."

The policeman fingered an indent on the dashboard. There was a moist crimson stain.

"Looky here," he said, extracting himself from the wreckage. He waved a pair of pliers. Secure in its grip was one of Suzanne Shackleford's bicuspids.

Seymour Barnes was abusing himself in the boathouse when he heard the screams. The others would assume he was stealing a nap, as was his custom those afternoons Brian Langdon was absent. Two months previous he'd responded to a Help Wanted sign posted at the front gate. He and his pal Herbie were driving by, sharing a joint, listening to one of Phil Frank's motivational CDs.

"Do yourself a favour, learn one new word per day," Frank was saying. "Get yourself a dictionary, leave it in the bathroom. At Success International we call this exercise a *vowel* movement."

Frank had been urging listeners to seize opportunities as they arise — like now, with this invitation of employment, Future Home of Shoreline Lodge.

"I'll wait in the truck," Herbie said.

Seymour had been put to work assisting tradesmen.

"You have to wear a hairnet if you want to keep that ponytail, son," Langdon had told him. "And those red sneakers don't belong on a construction site. You need steel-toed boots."

The cries began again just as Seymour was about to spill. It sounded like Theodora, the Shackleford's Filipina housekeeper. He zipped up and ran to the house. Langdon was barking into a walkie-talkie. Workers had converged in the driveway.

"It's Suzanne!" Theodora cried. "She's being airlifted to Cobalt General!"

A van pulled onto the property. Barry, Kenji, and Theodora clambered into the back seat.

"Everybody else, back to work," Langdon ordered. "We've still got a deadline to meet."

Seymour waited until the contractor was out of sight before returning to the boathouse. Success International encouraged students to finish what they start.

Sergeant Al Watson of the Cobalt Community Constabulary rose early for the drive to Rail Spur. There were posters to distribute at restaurants and service stations along the way; fugitives had been sighted in the vicinity. He also wanted to inquire about cruise prices at the marina. The Police Benevolent Association had its annual do coming up.

And then there was the matter of Norval Spikes. Watson had heard his old friend was considering early retirement, something about leaving policing to start a private security firm. If the rumour was accurate, his job would be up for grabs. Al's wife Merna had always wanted to live in Rail Spur.

Years earlier he and Norval had been classmates in the Justice program at Cobalt Community College and enforcers on the school's ice hockey team, he patrolling the left wing, Norval the right. The Cannonballs placed last in the league standings but proudly led in penalty minutes.

Watson followed the police chief into his office. He asked about the cruises and Norval tossed out a few price guestimates. As for the security firm, nothing had been finalized.

"You wouldn't believe the number of break-ins, Al," he said. "Folks are screaming for private muscle."

Norval was studying the poster of the fugitive Patti Markham.

"They really want to get that one," Watson said. "More serious charges are pending."

"Sure is a pretty thing. What did she do?"

"She's suspected of — "

The reply was lost to a commotion in the hallway. A couple of uniforms were wrestling an aboriginal youth to the floor. One of the constables subdued the boy with a headlock. His partner handcuffed him to an overhead pipe.

Al and Norval joined the others in the hallway.

"This spear chucker giving you fellas a hard time?" Norval said.

"We found a wallet in the Lincoln he was driving, chief. It identifies the owner as an investment banker."

Norval gave the suspect's hair a fatherly ruffle — then drove a meaty fist into his abdomen. The boy turned pale, then vomited. One of the officers opened a window.

"That's for allowing interest rates to rise," the chief said, chuckles all around.

Every summer visitors reported to police the disappearance of a cherished family pet. We let him out for just a sec, they'd swear. Children wailed inconsolably. Police Chief Spikes was flummoxed. Ditto the town's vet. When a producer from a Cobalt TV station began snooping around, *Record* publisher Ed Leatherdale had Harry pen an editorial blaming the jackals, of which, in the hills, there were believed to be many.

In all the years Harry had resided in Rail Spur, he'd never seen a jackal. He'd heard that an early European visitor had brought a dozen in for the dogfights, and that several had escaped their holding pens. Some people said they had mated with the wolves.

"The benefits of reinstituting a bounty on these creatures should not be scoffed at," he wrote. "A cull worked in the previous century. No reason it wouldn't in this one."

But there had never been a cull. Ed said that if a story is repeated often enough, people begin to believe it; he'd seen it dozens of times. And he was right. Free-spending hunters spared no expense trying to bag one of the elusive beasts.

Seymour was hugging the bar in the Last Call, thinking about his girl, Angelina. Though they'd lived together for several months, he still didn't know much about her. He'd noticed her up on the highway one day in her LA Dodgers club jacket and offered her a lift into town. Another college girl looking to waitress for the summer, he figured. He recommended she talk to George Elliott at the Dollar Store.

"My name," she said, fixing him from behind turquoise contact lenses, "is Angelina DuBois." She printed it in large letters on an invisible blackboard. "It's French."

Seymour's cabin was a dozen kilometres east of town, just beyond the Blackberry Hills Indian Reservation. He'd been living there with Nitro, his irritable German shepherd, and, until he passed, his Uncle Roy.

He and Herbie moved to the billiards table. Seymour racked the balls; Herbie studied the Wanted poster.

"Your shot," Seymour said.

Herbie stabbed the poster with his cue.

"She sorta looks like Angelina," he said.

"That chick has long brown hair," Seymour said. "Angelina's, in case you haven't noticed, is collar-length; she's a dirty blond. That one's got green eyes; Angie's are turquoise blue. And her name ain't Markham, it's DuBois, which is French. Fuck, you're stupid."

Seymour wasn't naïve enough to think that what he and Angelina had was love. Before her arrival there had been only Betty NoLastName, from the reservation. Each visit cost him twenty dollars and never lasted longer than it took to smoke a cigarette. Once or twice he was left with festering sores requiring medical attention.

Uncle Roy had believed a woman was like Tullaine Lake: unpredictable, subject to moods. A few years back they'd been out trolling early in the AM, an hour they knew the largemouth bass to be ravenous.

"Losing all that blood every month," Roy had said, rolling one of the cigarettes that would kill him. "You or I, we'd be dead in a jiffy. Best not to trust 'em."

Besides Betty and Uncle Roy, the sum of what Seymour knew about the opposite sex had been gleaned from magazines and porn videos. There was a one-night stand now and then, always the ugliest girl in the bar, a leftover. He also learned a few things from snooping on college girls who believed they'd discovered a secluded beach where they could take it all off, anything for a tan. Seymour had heard some kind of expert on TV tell Oprah that when two people fall in love their hearts palpitate, their knees wobble. The man claimed it was a medical fact; someone had done tests.

Neither palpitating heart nor wobbly knees ever occurred to Seymour. What he and Angelina had was a mutual convenience. She had rent-free accommodations and transportation every morning to George Elliott's Dollar Store. As for him, having Angelina at home was like a case of beer in the fridge, there for the taking.

And he had his box. It was made of steel. He carried the key on a shoelace looped around his neck. He slept with the key. He swam with it. Even when he was shagging Betty, he'd wear the key.

There were two photos in the box. The first was of Uncle Roy and Nitro as a pup, the only family he'd ever known. The second photo was of a beautiful woman. Seymour believed it might be the mother he'd never known.

In the beginning Angelina had shared his enthusiasm for Success International, but she soon began slipping off to the bedroom to study her cosmetology worksheets. She told him that first day that her career aspiration was to work as a makeup "artiste" on movie sets.

"Squirrels," she'd say, "couldn't live on what George pays me."

Angelina used balloons to practise her makeup technique. On some she inserted exaggerated lashes, on others she sketched beauty spots and dimples. She attached her balloons to the walls to escape Nitro, who was spooked by these intruders, mauling them at every opportunity. Whenever the dog did manage to sink a fang into one, the blast startling Angelina, she always issued the same admonition.

"The mutt will live to regret that."

One of the made-up balloons was fastened to the lamp above their bed. It would swoop and spin in the draught blowing through the cabin, all the while looking at Seymour — looking right through him, it sometimes seemed. When the balloon reached the end of its line the head would snap back, the way he supposed a condemned head would at a lynching.

Nights he couldn't sleep, Seymour would listen to Phil Frank on his earphones. He particularly enjoyed the third CD, a live performance in some hotel ballroom. Frank allows for a long pause after an ovation, then says, "Everyone has his or her moment, the winning hand. You either risk everything or fold and go home."

Seymour wondered how long he'd have to wait for his winning hand. He didn't know why, it was just a feeling, but he didn't believe he had long.

"The internal injuries," the doctor was telling them, "are not as bad as we had originally assumed. However . . ."

Barry and Kenji snivelled on one side of the bed; Theodora did likewise on the other.

"Her scans show normal brain function," the doctor said, adjusting a bank of blinking monitors. "We won't know more until she regains consciousness."

Suzanne lay still as a corpse. Bandages concealed the damage. Theodora didn't feel up to visiting Cedar Ridge

Retreat, where Granny Shackleford, the clan matriarch, resided. Although returned to the care of her grandchildren for the occasional weekend, the old woman hadn't uttered a word since suffering a stroke several years earlier. No point upsetting her.

The doctor said, "The greatest damage is to the bones in her face."

The visitors gasped. That million dollar face, agents used to call it.

"The jaw, eye sockets, nose, and cheekbones have been shattered. Think of a chandelier crashing to the floor."

There was a chandelier in the Shackleford dining room. They all tried imagining it falling, the mess.

"What about cosmetic surgery?" Barry asked. "Can anything be done?"

The doctor backed out of the room. "Let's have that talk after we've done the reconstructive work."

On the drive home a squall swept in from the north. Raindrops bounced off the winding asphalt road. In the back seat Theodora released the blue ribbon from her hair, twining it tightly around her fingers.

Patti's cellmate had tattoos inked into every limb. The letters on each finger of her left hand were most visible when she made a fist: BUTCH. Her underarm hair was braided.

Everybody called her Mr. President.

"Shed them clothes," she decreed that first day. "Let's sample the merchandise."

Patti figured her new roommate possessed more testosterone than boyfriends she'd had, so what was required to survive in the Correctional Centre for Women wasn't nearly as difficult as some sensitive types might suppose. Besides, some of the props the girls smuggled inside did a decent job of bridging the differences. Whoever wore the champ's LA Dodger jacket was the "first lady."

The counsellors, the guards, the probation officers, the pamphlets they were always leaving on the meal trays said much the same to Patti as Phil Frank and Success International said to Seymour: do this, don't do that. She had no problem convincing people she'd take their advice. But she, Patti Markham, was programmed differently. She liked to do things her way.

Mr. President passed every free moment in the gym. Had to, she said, if she wanted to rule. Patti worked in the prison hair salon. She calculated that with good behaviour she'd be sprung in two years; that is, as long as they didn't find out about the other stuff.

Each tier had a trustee. Usually the job went to an older inmate who scheduled showers and handed out bedding. The trustee on Patti's tier was French Canadian. Her name was Angelina DuBois.

"Gonna be waiting for me when my time's up, babe?" Patti's protector would ask, lights out, the couple curled up in the top bunk.

"You have to ask?"

The dialogue, repeated verbatim most evenings, had the effect of a double Valium on the cellblock despot.

Moments later, tons of iron pumped, Mr. President was snoring vociferously.

At the beginning of Patti's second year, eight inmates devised an escape plan: out the laundry window, across the roof of the administration building, a drop to the perimeter. They waited for a moonless night. A fight over TV programming diverted the screws. Most of the girls ran toward town; Patti, Mr. President, and another dyke named Larry made for the mountains. The latter were guessing the dogs would follow the former, which turned out to be the case. A week later, bedraggled and mosquito-bitten, the trio stumbled out of the bush and onto the highway. A trucker transported the fugitives west. They paid for the mileage with Patti's charms.

In a farmer's field outside Cobalt, Mr. President and Larry got into a fight over the remaining cheese and baloney sandwich. The pair settled the dispute with a jailhouse contest called Last Man Standing. The rules were self-explanatory: the two of them toe-to-toe, one swing per round, winner take all — Patti and the sandwich. With Larry's face in the mud and Mr. President nursing a broken wrist, the first lady up and abdicated.

"I'm gonna find you, girl!" Patti, fleeing through the woods, heard her cellmate proclaim. "Once the property of Mr. President, always the property!"

The paper at the printer, Ed Leatherdale was explaining to Harry the reason a follow-up story on Suzanne Shackleford was unsuitable for the *Record*.

"This isn't some fancy magazine," he said, and not for the first time. "We do local news, sandlot sports, and fishing tips."

At the far end of the office, Archie and Sandi were pretending not to listen.

"This is a story of how a fashion model deals with disfigurement, Ed. When did we stop printing human interest?"

The publisher exhaled wearily.

"I'm hoping Shoreline Lodge will generate some advertising dollars before everything goes digital. If we piss off the Shacklefords, we won't see a dime."

"You mean to say," Harry said, "that we can't lose anything if we don't report anything?"

Ed's lip curled into a sneer. "You're learning, Harry."

The exchange reminded the reporter why he'd always kept a resignation letter on file. He'd bent more than one ear regarding his dissatisfaction, informing anyone who'd listen — some of whom tattled — that the publisher had been handed the newspaper by his old man. Ed could neither type nor spell.

Ed refused to run articles reflecting negatively on personal friends, town luminaries, potential advertisers or well-heeled tourists. The wrongdoings of trailer park residents and aboriginals filled the news pages.

"It's the way of the world," he would say. "I didn't make the rules."

These rules allowed him to accept whatever favours were offered for his spinning of public perceptions, which included — twice — his being named Rail Spur Citizen of the Year.

"Anybody doesn't like working here," he huffed, "there's the door."

After lunch Harry deleted the resignation letter. The new draft would more accurately reflect present sentiments.

"Your Royal Dickhead," it began.

The meeting with the family lawyer Cornell Westmore was set for noon. With Suzanne in hospital, signing authority for Shackleford business was being temporarily turned over to sibling Barry. Record temperatures were prophesied, so Theodora opened the umbrella on the veranda and hurried back inside to spoon out the ice cream.

"He's here," Barry said.

Cornell stepped from a taxi just as the clock in the study tolled. He'd been handling the family's affairs for as long as anyone could remember. His wife Babs, suffering the final stages of Alzheimer's, was a resident of the same facility caring for Granny Shackleford. As far as anyone could determine, the two old friends were oblivious of their mutual residency.

"Join us, Theo," Cornell said. "After all these years, I'd say you qualify as family."

Offering shade to the assembly was an expansive cherry tree. At its base lay a heap of clothes. Kenji was perched high in its clutches. He was playing his flute.

The lawyer arranged several folders on the table.

"The surgery went well," he said.

"Is she in much pain?" asked Theodora.

"We were able to chat for about fifteen minutes before Suzanne got groggy. She seemed mentally alert, though. We can all visit in a few days."

"What did she say about the lodge?" Barry asked.

"She wants the project on hold, not cancelled. I just got off the phone with Brian Langdon. He's disappointed, naturally, but he's assured me the time can be made up next spring. He recommended you hire someone to keep an eye on the equipment."

"We already have," Barry said, waving at Seymour, just then guiding a wheelbarrow through the yard.

"He's a good boy," Theodora said.

Cornell peered above his horn-rims.

"I believe legal aid represented him a few times. Misdemeanours, as I recall."

"He's a little odd," Barry acknowledged, "but nothing's gone missing. We're going to keep him on; this old house needs some maintenance."

The taxi returned; the driver brayed its horn. Barry initialled the final document, and everyone spooned the last of their ice cream.

"A friend?" Cornell inquired, a glance up the cherry tree.

"Kenji's a language student from Japan," Barry said.

The old man eased himself into the back seat of the taxi and rolled down the window.

"This Kenny fellow," he said. "Can't he play something a little more cheerful?"

Herbie went over the side just off Wigwam Rock, minnows skittering furtively through the beam of his spotlight. He didn't like staying down long, so he only carried the one tank. Liquid wasn't his element. If something went wrong he couldn't solve the problem with a corrective smack. He'd boosted the diving gear off a tourist. The boat had belonged to a local he didn't care for.

He ploughed the sand with a long-bladed knife, stuffing into a sack what he thought could be peddled or traded. Tonight's booty included a cigarette lighter and an assortment of coins. He emptied his find onto the floor of the boat. A bracelet caught his eye. Perhaps he'd get something for it. If not, he could always give it to one of the boys from Blackberry Hills. They were like dogs, always chasing shiny objects.

Harry didn't have any trouble finding a publication interested in the Suzanne Shackleford story. He settled on *Glitter*; its office was on the coast. The magazine was a slick, perfumed monthly whose subscribers would be familiar with the former model. When she was starting out, top agencies had employed her to flog credit cards and mutual funds, automobiles and foreign vacations. The editor, Anthony Telford, felt her frequent appearances in the ads would lend a unique dimension to the piece.

"It has a kind of Humpty Dumpty appeal," he told Harry. "Some of our subscribers buy the magazine for the ads. They see a page of copy, they get drowsy. Attach the right photo, some might actually try reading this."

Harry didn't inform Telford he hadn't yet approached Suzanne about her participation. Nurses at Cobalt General had told him their celebrity patient wasn't talking. So far, the only one saying anything was Cornell.

"I'm afraid that lovely face is no more," the lawyer had said, unaware of Harry's desire to author her story. "We'll have to wait and see if she can be put back together again."

Behind the cedar hedges lining the driveway. On a mattress under the porch. In the garden shed. In the attic. Seymour had even come across Barry's gay friends coupling in a child's tree house. With Suzanne in hospital, they usually arrived in the morning and were still frolicking when Seymour left for home in the evening.

They sunbathed on the beach or lounged around the pool. Couples strolled the grounds, daisies in their hair. Some snorted cocaine as greedily as children devouring sweets. When he first stumbled across two groping men, he apologized and fled. A few days later, the shock abating, he watched from the woods.

How that must hurt, he thought.

Despite her evangelical leanings, Theodora seemed unfazed by the boys. When a guest spent too much time in the sun, she would nurse him. Heartbroken? She listened. "That's just the way they are," she told Seymour. "We're all God's children."

At any time of the day he could hear their rutting. They squealed, fought, sang, cried out. They danced, wrestled on the lawn, and played high-heel badminton. Theatricals were staged requiring elaborate costuming. The pairings, Seymour noted, were never the same for long: intimates one day, acquaintances the next. Barry loaned Kenji like a library book.

Neighbours complained that the partygoers depressed real estate values. Seymour had heard some rowdies at the Last Call refer to them as "Brownies." In time their antics ceased to offend him. Like Theo, he even learned to appreciate their company. They understood he was not one of them and let him be. Still, he was careful not to flaunt a bare chest.

One day, the boys at siesta, the Shackleford house-keeper invited Seymour to lunch. They sat at the oak table in the dining room, curtains billowing around them like the loose folds of a gown. Through the open window he could smell blossoms ripening on an ancient magnolia tree. Seymour told Theodora about life on Tullaine Lake before the tourists arrived, about the tarpaper shacks and the frigid dash to an outhouse every morning. She told him about the Philippines and the ribbons she wore in her hair.

"My granddaughter sent me seven," she said. "One for each day of the week."

Seymour never forgot that lunch. It was the magnolia blossoms, their scent wafting through the rooms on the balmy summer breeze. He always knew if a magnolia was nearby. Even when out walking at night. It was like a woman hiding in the dark: betrayed by her perfume.

The reporting job at the *Record* was Sandi's first since completing the college journalism program. From the very start Harry, who doubled as the editor, treated her with contempt. She was Ed's niece, after all. Harry kept the byline stories for himself and assigned her press releases and minor announcements. He and the publisher sniped at each other like embittered old women.

Harry would begin each day as though he was performing a ritual. He'd arrive at the office, a take-out espresso in hand, at 9 AM, not a greeting for anyone. More often than not he was hungover. He'd sit down in front of his computer screen and say aloud, as though uttering a prayer, "Same words, different order."

There were plenty of mistakes in the stories the girl filed that summer. Harry often rearranged her paragraphs and rewrote many of her sentences. "Your opening," he told her, "should make me cry or make me horny." On the filing cabinet next to her desk he had Scotch-taped a hand-lettered sign: THE ONLY STUPID QUESTION IS THE ONE YOU DON'T ASK.

He bristled when the girl told him about the rental apartment she'd found. How she had never lived on her own. He wasn't interested in her poor-little-rich-girl whine. She told him about the clerk at the Dollar Store, a girl named Angelina who seemed to know exactly what Sandi would need to furnish her place. They were the same age — might they become friends? Such chatter went in one of Harry's ears and out the other. You're getting your own place, you've met a new friend — what the fuck do I care?

"Are there really jackals in these hills?" she asked him.

"I don't know about jackals in the hills," he said, "but there are plenty of assholes in town."

II

Suzanne spent the remainder of the summer and much of the fall enduring several surgeries. Just as the first snow began swirling in the December sky, she was released from hospital. The homecoming party consisted of Barry, Theo, and Kenji. Seymour had been asked to drive. The mountains that day appeared as they always did under grey skies, like the spine of a great, slumbering beast.

Suzanne asked Seymour to park the van at a rest stop on the highway. Canada geese had landed on a frozen pond. As the others scattered birdseed, Seymour stole a glance at his bandaged employer. There were openings in the gauze for her eyes, ears, nostrils, and mouth. He wondered what a fright the one-time beauty must be unwrapped.

"We always complain about the visitors," Suzanne said. "They can be such a bloody nuisance, but I always feel sad when they're gone. It's like a wonderful party coming to an end."

Once home, he watched her climb the front steps without assistance and survey the grounds from the veranda. Barry's friends had been swept away like bread crumbs. Even wounded, he noticed, Suzanne's bearing was regal: shoulders back, head angled just so.

"The place looks good," she said.

As work on the lodge resumed, Seymour conveyed blueprints and other documents between Brian Langdon's headquarters in Cobalt and Suzanne's home office. He also drove her to weekly sessions with the therapist Arlene Jamieson, who had an office on the pier. In the beginning she preferred sitting alone in the van's back seat, occasionally commenting on the weather or a passing landmark. He kept his replies short, always the employee, as Phil Frank recommended.

Gradually, though, she opened up. Her laugh, an infectious chortle unmistakably her own, had survived the accident. She told him that once Granny succumbed, an occurrence whispered to be imminent, she and Barry would inherit everything.

"What does one do," she mused, "with everything?"

Seymour offered to drive her to the mall in Cobalt — to anywhere she wanted — but she declined.

"I'm used to people staring at me," she said, "but for different reasons."

He reminded her that many heroes shielded their identities.

"Zorro, Batman, the Lone Ranger . . . "

And then one day it happened. Right out of the blue, just as Phil Frank had promised on the third CD. *Everyone has his or her moment, the winning hand. You either risk everything or fold and go home.*

His moment, he explained to Angelina, was "in two parts. It has to be assembled like Ikea furniture: each part on its own, nothing. Together, magic.

"You're not making sense," she said. "Nothing new about that."

So he reminded her of the night they were channel surfing. A comedy rerun, the halftime show of a football game. A filmmaker explaining the process that unfolds when a patron enters a darkened theatre.

"Like the guy said, most of what we see in movies is unbelievable. We'd never accept these things if they were happening in real life. When a car flips five times, the driver can't crawl out and run off. One man can't destroy a dozen adversaries with a few slaps. It's a suspension of disbelief. In a movie, something happens. It's like a silent — what's the word — collaboration, right?"

"So?"

"So the first part was the suspension of disbelief," he says. "Here's the second part: Barry is worried about Suzanne," he said. "She seems depressed. A boyfriend has stopped calling. The doctor said the gauze wrap is no longer necessary, but she won't let anyone see her without it. There's going to be a get-together. The usual bunch: Theo, Barry, Kenji, Cornell, me. Even Grandma. You help cater the affair."

"Why?"

"You'll see."

Everyone at the party praised Angelina's figure, her complexion, how good she and Seymour seemed together. After the dishes were done Suzanne insisted Angelina join the party. Seymour recorded the festivities with a disposable camera he'd nicked from the Dollar Store.

A week later, the photos developed, he spread out the images.

"Look," he told her. "You and Suzanne are about the same height, and you're both thin. Under the bandages, Suzanne's face has gone. No one knows what she'll look like *after* the cosmetic surgery. People are expecting her to look different."

Angelina remained quiet as Seymour explained his plan. When he was finished, she said, "Let me see if I've got this right: You want me to quit my job and hide out here at the cabin while you move into the guest house. I'm going to have cosmetic surgery. You're going to explain my disappearance by saying we broke up. You're going to supply me with letters, cards, photos, family histories. I'm going to do my hair like her, learn how to walk and talk like her. That's nuts. You expect me to *laugh* like her?"

"We have to convince everyone who knows her to suspend disbelief," Seymour said. "If we can do that, everything will be ours."

"Yeah, after you murder her."

"Wrong," Seymour said. "After *we* murder her."

"This plan of yours," Angelina said. "It sounds like a movie script."

"Really? Thanks."

"A really *stupid* movie script."

Sergeant Watson left his car at the marina. A couple of kids fishing for flounders pointed out the cruise operator. After a quick inspection the policeman handed the skipper a cheque in the amount agreed upon. The Police Benevolent Association would hold its outing the first weekend in August.

The poster of Patti Markham had been bothering him. It had been on the bulletin board in the Cobalt detachment since the prison break. A call logged on the tip line said the girl in the poster resembled one of the sales clerks at the Dollar Store. Nabbing the fugitive would endear him to Rail Spur's town council, something he was hoping they'd remember when considering the chief's replacement.

The Dollar Store sign swayed in the breeze above the sidewalk. Watson waited until the sales clerk had finished with a customer.

"Patti Markham?"

The girl turned. "There's nobody here by that name, sorry."

He found George Elliott stocking shelves. He showed him a snapshot the inmate had left behind in her cell, a tattooed bicep draped around her neck.

"Hey," George said. "That's Angelina. She quit a while back. Is she okay?"

He used the ruse about the girl receiving an inheritance if she could be located. He said there was some confusion about the name.

"Angelina DuBois," said George. "It's French."

Harry was the Last Call's final patron. On the drive home he pulled over to the side of the road and passed out. In the morning he relieved himself at a picnic site. It was a fluke he spotted the bandaged Suzanne Shackleford passing in Seymour's pickup.

The drive to the airport normally took about ninety minutes. Seymour watched Suzanne fiddle with her bracelet. She had been fitted with a customized mask, a plastic facial mould. If she was going to cover up until the cosmetic work was complete, she might as well be comfortable.

"Scared?" he asked. Her last operation was scheduled for the following day. Piece by piece, Humpty Dumpty was being reassembled.

"A little."

He hadn't secured Suzanne's luggage; the suitcases collided in the truck bed at every bend in the road. Two kilometres east of town he swerved onto a gravel road.

"Shortcut," he said. "I'll stop soon and take care of the suitcases."

Harry returned to his car and called the office. Archie picked up.

"Can you see the town map from where you are?" Harry asked. "Second exit east of town, where's it lead?"

The copy boy ran his finger over the map.

"Dead end, eventually. Used to be a quarry out there; kids swam in it after the rains. They filled it in when one of them drowned."

The pickup was travelling so fast the door panels rattled.

"Slow down, please," Suzanne said. "We've got lots of time."

Seymour took his foot off the accelerator; the pickup rolled to a stop.

"I'd better tie down that luggage."

Harry's headache returned, and his bowels were bursting. While squatting in the bushes he heard three loud blasts — *boom! boom! boom!* If nothing else the drive had resulted in an idea for a feature, Out of Season Hunting: Is the Problem Getting Worse? The story could run as this weekend's special feature.

III

When Seymour's truck swept up the driveway Barry was lounging by the pool and Theo was hanging laundry.

"Well?" Suzanne said, sliding from the truck. *"Voila!"*

"My darling Suzanne," said Theo. "You look . . . gorgeous!"

The pivotal moment of the plan passed without incident; there was no turning back. Barry had never been a concern. Most mornings, all those drugs, he probably couldn't even recognize himself in the mirror. Following a cup of tea, Suzanne feigned fatigue and retired to her room. Around midnight, Seymour called her from the guesthouse.

"Told ya," he said.

But success could not be claimed until the new face had been paraded past all who'd known Suzanne.

"You are cordially invited," announced the invitation, "to a sneak preview of Rail Spur's most exclusive holiday resort." Inside was an artist's rendering of a completed Shoreline Lodge; it would be built adjacent to the house.

Chaos reigned in the days leading up to the event. Service folk came and went. Seymour was fitted for a tux. Jasmine was in bloom and torches had been posted throughout the grounds. A jazz combo played in the garden.

The hostess stood at an upstairs window. Already into his medicines, Barry insisted on trying to announce the guests: the *Record* publisher Ed Leatherdale and his niece Sandi; town councillors; Gordon Lungren, Rail Spur Savings & Loan; Granny . . .

Theo was joined on the veranda by Norval, wearing civies.

"Never thought I'd see the day," he said, indicating the dancers.

Barry waltzed by. In his arms was a miniskirted Oriental girl.

"Great legs," said the chief. "And all this time I thought . . . "

Later, a breeze flitting through the garden, the hostess appeared unannounced. Guests collected as she descended the stairs. She squeezed hands and dispensed compliments.

"I'm so pleased you could make it," she said. "Thank you all for coming."

Matrons teared up. Men were smitten.

The hostess whispered in Harry's ear, "Cornell has told me about the article you're proposing. You might have talked to me first."

After the last of the guests had left, Seymour and the hostess retreated to the beach. The indigo sky was ablaze with stars.

"Well," he said, draining a beer, "I'd say that went well."

She kicked off her heels and hoisted her gown, wading knee deep into the water. And then she tossed her hair and laughed heartily, a perfect Suzanne.

Over the following weeks and months friends and neighbours were invited to the house. Seymour marvelled at how Angelina, the reluctant participant in his plot, had everyone bamboozled. The months she'd spent rehearsing at the cabin had not been wasted. She remembered faces, names, shared experiences. He had written the score; she was performing it masterfully.

Anyone believing the new face didn't resemble the old one — and it didn't, not really, despite the talented Dr. Beaverstock in his fancy office on the coast — was too polite to say so. Besides, the new face wasn't supposed to match the old one; it was the genius of the plan.

Only Grandma seemed skeptical. At their first meeting following the unveiling she rolled her eyes and fidgeted. Driving her back to the care home that night, Seymour pulled over to the side of the road and switched off the engine.

"Try that again," he said, "and I'll wheel you into the woods and leave you for the jackals."

The rebuilt Suzanne quickly became a subject of interest in Rail Spur, so Seymour persuaded Barry to accompany his sister on a few courtesy calls, George Elliott at the Dollar Store being one of them.

"He's as dense as a shower curtain," she said. "Put a wig on his own mother and he wouldn't know her."

Brother and sister sipped lattes at Café Casa and wine at The Last Call. A hush greeted their entrance at both venues; an eruption of chatter followed their departures. Flushed with the success of her day, Angelina joined Seymour at the guest house later that evening. But she declined his invitation to stay over.

"We're business partners now," she said, slipping his embrace. "Let's not complicate things."

"Whatever," he replied. "It's time for my dip."

As he did most summer nights, Seymour dropped off the end of the dock and swam to a small island in the middle of the lake. He'd remain there until he felt strong enough to return.

According to the plan, Barry was next. For months Herbie had been boosting prescription medications from tourists. Seymour had been grinding the pills into a powder and sprinkling it like sugar on Barry's Fruit Loops. He was now spending hours on the toilet every day, yet he remained very much alive.

"I don't understand it," Seymour grumbled. "He's already swallowed enough poison to stop an elephant."

Angelina was disturbed by Herbie's involvement in the plan; Seymour sensed she disliked half-breeds. She also didn't care for his aftershave or his buttercup yellow Volkswagen; both attracted too much attention. She was especially bothered by his interest in little boys.

"Kids grow up," she told Seymour. "Some of them go to the cops. Others get revenge."

"We have to think like management," Seymour said. "Herbie is exactly what we need. Short-term contract work, a grunt. After Barry, we'll cut him loose."

The heiress, as scheduled, knocked on Gordon Lungren's office door at 2 PM. The branch manager of Rail Spur Savings & Loan was at the window, admiring his sailboat, the largest vessel in the marina.

"I'll never forget that party on your boat," she cackled, dropping into a chair. "I don't recall ever having laughed so hard. That's not a good idea on a full stomach."

"Especially," Lungren played along, "on a swaying sailboat."

The banker voiced his disappointment with her decision to cancel the project; a five-star resort would have been good for the town. His assistant, Marion Wellington, handed her the papers.

"The accident made me think about the important things in life," she offered. "Does the world really need another resort?"

She felt Lungren studying her as she signed and returned the documents. Marion glanced cursorily at the signature before leading her to a cubicle and three safety deposit boxes. When there was no more room in her satchel, Suzanne requested a large bag.

Seymour stashed most of his share of the loot in his steel box. He hid it up a fir tree behind the cabin.

Herbie woke from his nap and rolled into a sitting position. A dental plate soaked in a glass of water. He slid the denture into his mouth and swallowed the H_2O.

"Ahh . . . "

There was a rap on the cabin door.

"It's me."

The boy's name was Melvin.

"Where's the dog?"

"In the shed, like you told me."

After he'd finished with Melvin, Herbie went to work on the pooch. Around midnight it was ready. He tore off a piece of hindquarter and dipped it into a tub of barbecue sauce.

"*Mmm.*" He passed a slice to the boy. "This would be yummy with mashed potatoes."

The partners made plans to mark their triumph in style. Angelina reserved a couple of hotel rooms on the coast. But just as they were leaving the house, Seymour received some bad news: Nitro, who'd been staying with Herbie, had been hit by a truck.

"I warned you about that animal," Angelina said.

"I figured he'd be safe up there," Seymour said.

He drove out to Blackberry Hills alone. There was an overturned fridge and a discarded mattress outside Herbie's trailer. Melvin was hosing down the Volkswagen.

"I'll show you where we buried him," Herbie said. "It's a real nice spot. I think it must have been a semi. Stay for a bite?"

Seymour declined — Angelina was waiting back at the house.

"It's stew," said Herbie. "I've got plenty."

Seymour caught a whiff and reconsidered.

"That looks familiar," he said of a bracelet hanging on the wall. "Where'd ya get it?"

"Don't recall," Herbie said, dishing out the grub. "Where I get everything else, probably: a parked car."

There was a boxing match on TV. The stew was gone before the TKO in the sixth.

"That hit the spot." Seymour belched. "What was it?"

"An old squaw recipe," Herbie said. "I figured you'd like it."

Harry was in the laundromat thumbing through the latest issue of *Glitter*. His whites had been dried and he was waiting on the last load. Enter Karen Le Duc. Harry had gotten chummy with the divorcee when he was still new in Rail Spur. They had groped each other once at a New Year's Eve party. But then he moved into a bungalow across town. Whenever they ran into each other, both pretended the party had never happened.

Karen did all the talking. Told him that her cousin Mavis had taken the same aerobics class at the rec centre as Stephanie Johns. And Stephanie Johns, she rattled on, Harry nodding off, was a relation by marriage to Marion Wellington, the personal assistant to Gordon Lungren at Rail Spur Savings & Loan.

" . . . and when she heard Shoreline Lodge wouldn't be built . . . "

Harry was back at the office making calls before his socks had dried.

"Did anyone else know the resort project had been canned? Why am I learning about this in the laundromat?"

Ed was out hustling ads.

"It's news to me," Archie said sleepily.

When he couldn't reach Cornell by phone, the reporter drove to Cedar Ridge Retreat. He found the old man playing solitaire in the cafeteria.

"Suzanne has undergone a profound change, Harry," Cornell said. "She wants to do something different with her life. Traumatic experiences can do that. I'm helping write the announcement."

Patients were being led across the lawn. Babs Westmore, eyes vacant, dressing gown stained with food droppings, trailed the others. Granny Shackleford sat slumped in her wheelchair.

Harry had believed the magazine story about Suzanne would redeem his sorry ass. He now worried about job security at the *Record*.

Intending to demand an explanation, he drove out to the Shackleford place, but Suzanne's car and the pickup belonging to the kid were both absent. A crater on the beach was all that remained of the resort project. The drive had given him the opportunity to reconsider his intention to confront Suzanne. If she chose not to talk to him, what would be accomplished by a showdown? It wouldn't be the first time an interview subject had bailed. Who knows, she might change her mind some day.

Before driving off he spotted a presence in the middle of the road.

"Jesus F. Christ!"

He released the hand brake; the Cherokee rolled forward to where he could better view the beast. Its coat was sleek, shiny; the expression was fearless, malignant. He reached for his camera, but when he refocused his attention on the road, it had vanished.

Fil, Seymour began.

He glanced at Phil Frank's poster thumbtacked to the wall.

Phil, he amended.

Angelina was painting a toenail.

"His secretary will take one look at your scrawl and toss it into the garbage," she scoffed.

He had checked out a library book modelling sample letters: Business, Employment, Regret, Congratulatory, etc. He gripped his pen and tried again, *I'd like to take this oportunity to thank you . . .*

150

Seymour believed the plan wouldn't have succeeded without Phil Frank's counsel. Had it not been for the CDs, he'd still be thieving from tourists, a Herbie.

"Drop him a note, say thanks," Angelina advised. "Try being normal for once."

Recently Seymour had begun carrying an attaché case filled with cash. It comforted him knowing that if the world suddenly descended into anarchy, he'd still have means. He carried the Smith & Wesson everywhere, too, just in case.

After the cash haul from the Savings & Loan, Seymour set aside his T-shirts and Levis. He began wearing a shirt and tie after work. He'd found a shop at Cobalt Mall that sold clip-ons. The salesman helped him select seven, just like Theo and her hair ribbons: a different colour for each day of the week.

He refocused on the letter: *You are welcome to visit . . .*

He'd come up with a new signature. He made the loops larger and added a swirl, like important people. He didn't have a middle name, so he invented one.

Your student at Success International, he concluded, *Seymour P. Barnes.*

Barry, meanwhile, was still breathing. And as long as he was, they were in danger. Should the Shackleford scion bump into the wrong person in town — the therapist, say — and should questions be asked, well . . .

"I think I might have something," Barry finally allowed, the first indication the medicines were working. "I feel kinda funny."

After ingesting a stranger's prescription with his breakfast cereal, Barry had become incoherent. He was perspiring heavily.

"Those sounds he's making," Seymour told Angelina. "It's like he's speaking in tongues."

But the next day Barry was . . . Barry. The latest batch of pills only made him poop.

In the beginning Seymour had been entertained by Barry's behaviour. He'd enjoyed wagering with Angelina which day would be his last. But they were growing restless. The plan couldn't proceed until the last heir had been eliminated. They also discussed Granny.

"She doesn't figure in the will," Seymour said. "Whoever inherits the estate becomes her guardian. Besides, she could croak any day."

"Wrinkles is a tough old broad," said Angelina. "Don't be surprised if she outlasts us all."

A few days later, a Sunday, Barry and Kenji entered a 7-Eleven east of Cobalt. Barry craved a jumbo bag of Doritos promising additional cheese. While passing the store, a retired hardware salesman driving home from a prayer breakfast suffered a massive coronary. His Buick Electra jumped the meridian. When the car finally came to rest, the old man was dead. His wife, nary a bone left unbroken, would spend the rest of her days wishing she were, too. Not a lick of Kenji's slicked-back hair had been disturbed. Barry had something in common with a snowfall: what remained of him had to be shovelled off the pavement.

At the funeral home Seymour elected to doze in the pickup. Albert Albertson, the director, greeted Angelina and led her to a brightly lit showroom.

About a dozen caskets were on display. They ranged from a sleek stainless steel capsule with silk pillowcases to a simple wooden container. With an imperious wave the businessman dispersed gossiping sales agents. He slid a folder under Angelina's arm.

"Our literature explains the savings, the specials and our guarantee of customer satisfaction."

"Unless you're a medium," she said, "I doubt the customer can be contacted."

The presentation ended where it began, alongside the costly capsule. Angelina returned to the pine box.

"This will do," she said.

Seymour and Angelina decided to lunch at a diner not far from where Barry had met his end. She never turned down an opportunity to eat out. Meals at the estate were prepared under the watchful eye of Theodora. Plenty of salads, no red meat. Fashion model food.

The woman at the counter was staring at them.

"Ring any bells?" Angelina asked.

"Gimme a sec, it'll come. Oh, yeah — Arlene what's-her-name, your therapist. Suzanne stopped going after about a dozen sessions; she was too busy with the project."

He stole another glimpse.

"Looks like she's dyed her hair and lost a bunch of weight."

With Seymour in the washroom, Arlene made her move.

"Suzanne? You look fabulous! I've been meaning to call you."

She slid into the booth without invitation.

"Arlene — remember?" the therapist said. "You aren't the first person who didn't recognize me!"

"Of course, Arlene!" Angelina said. "You look wonderful." Then she blurted, "It was nice to see you," and awkwardly exited.

"You're gonna have to excuse her," said Seymour, back from the loo. He tossed a tip on the table. "Heard about Barry? The funeral is Saturday."

Perspiration beaded on his upper lip.

"These things take time," Arlene said.

He noticed her spying the remains of Angelina's cheeseburger.

IV

Two limos left the estate under a fine autumn drizzle. Herbie was driving the first; it contained Barry's Buick-bludgeoned body. The following vehicle transported a stoned Seymour Barnes, the grieving housekeeper Theodora, a vacant Grandma Shackleford, the one-tune flautist Kenji, and the woman everyone assumed to be the heartbroken sister Suzanne. All but Wrinkles wore sunglasses. She had cataracts.

Tullaine Meadows, their destination that morning, was located midway to the summit of Eagle Ridge

Mountain. The adjoining chapel, the crematorium, and the "meadows" were all owned by funeral director Albert Albertson.

Soon, huddled beneath umbrellas, were the solicitor Cornell Westmore, the banker Gordon Lungren, the police chief Norval Spikes, and the therapist Arlene Jamieson.

In the second row sat the newspaper publisher Ed Leatherdale and his niece Sandi, the reporter Harry Shapka, and the *Record* copy boy, Archie Meeks. The most stylishly attired, in their first appearance in more than a year, were Barry's playmates.

"We are gathered here today to bid farewell . . . "

The ceremony, like the deceased's troubled life, was brief. Soon the procession was retracing its route along the narrow mountain road.

After the reception, Seymour, Angelina and Herbie met back at the guest house to smoke a block of hashish Herbie had found in one of the cars.

"Which one?" Angelina asked, trapping the first hit in her lungs.

"Piece of shit Toyota," Herbie said. "Blue."

"Archie Meeks," Seymour said. "A dink."

They retired that evening believing their final problem solved.

Angelina enjoyed driving Barry's Jag. There were roads in the hills that hadn't held a tire in years. She knew of no sensation more exhilarating than a car sliding sideways as it entered a turn. It was like orgasm: control forfeited.

Back at the house, the plan was facing its first serious test.

"We have to call the police!" Theo shouted. "Before she gets back!"

Seymour had never seen the housekeeper in such a state.

"That's not Suzanne!" she cried. "I knew something wasn't right the minute she got back from the hospital! I tried telling myself it couldn't be true!"

Theo was able to stop crying just long enough to explain herself. "I know it sounds crazy, but Suzanne didn't talk that way. She wouldn't say those terrible things!"

"The accident affected her brain," Seymour said. "The doctor said so."

"But what about the food?" she said.

"The food?"

"This one eats anything! Our Suzanne is a vegetarian!"

"Have you told anyone else?"

"At the reception she was drinking iced tea. I heard her complain about a sensitive tooth." She squeezed his arm. "Suzanne has dental implants!"

Seymour paced. Theo flinched every time a car passed the property.

"Let me look into it," he said. "We don't want her thinking we suspect something."

"It's my turn to clean the tabernacle," she said. "It'll keep my mind off things."

An hour later Seymour was unloading Theo's cleaning supplies in the churchyard.

"The police will know what to do, don't worry."

Theo dug her nails into his arm. "But what have they done," she whimpered, "with my Suzanne?"

He went to her room early the next morning.

"Is that you, Seymour?"

He whispered, "Norval wants us to act like nothing's happened."

She opened the door and waved him inside. He studied Theo's modest living quarters. There was a cross above the bed, a porcelain statue of Jesus on a side table. Most people bring more to a picnic.

"Stay put," he said. "The chief is waiting on reinforcements."

"I'll wear the green ribbon today," she said. "For good luck."

"Theo?" called Angelina from the foot of the stairs. "You there? I want to see you in the TV room."

She heard Theo tapping a number into her cellphone. Angelina retraced her steps and turned on the TV. A moment later Theo was downstairs, shuffling along the hall. In the TV room she straightened the drapes, pounded dust from a cushion.

"Theo, we have a beautiful old lamp in the basement. Do you know the one I mean? It would look nice in this room."

The light bulb at the back of the basement had been unscrewed; Angelina felt her way in the dark. A spiderweb tickled her cheek. She found Theo beside the furnace. A shaft of daylight from a narrow service window exposed a hand, some leg, a length of green ribbon.

A car pulling in off the highway, an idling motor, the exhaust pipe perforated. A door slams, then a second. Muffled voices. A man and a woman.

"There aren't many places like this left," he says. "Nice."

In the basement, blood puddles on the concrete floor. The doorbell sounds like a loon keening from the far side of the lake.

"We're here to see Mr. Seymour Barnes," the man says. "My name is Phil Frank. This is my companion, Iris."

"Seymour went fishing," Angelina says. "He won't be back for hours."

"His wife, I presume?"

"His employer," she corrects.

Angelina hears a moan from the basement.

"This will explain our visit," Phil says, handing over the letter. Angelina recognizes the child-like script. *I would be onored . . . You are corduly invited . . . Please come anytime.*

Iris says, "We're about to begin a new production. Mr. Barnes expressed an interest in investing."

Theo cries out.

"My dog," Angelina says. "She just had a litter."

"Mr. Frank loves dogs," Iris says.

"I'll mention your visit to Mr. Barnes."

"We're staying at — "

Angelina ushers them back to their car. She returns quickly to the house.

The door leading to the basement squeaks open. An angry foot sends the housekeeper tumbling backwards.

At the Evangelical Four Square Tabernacle, Reverend Reginald McCarthy greets the visitor by bounding down the aisle and extending a hand.

"Welcome to the House of the Lord, Mr. . . . ?"

"Theodora's friend," Seymour says. "I drive her every Sunday, remember?"

The preacher slips on his glasses. "Of course, yes."

Seymour hands over a stack of Theo's religious pamphlets.

"Theodora had to return to the Philippines," he says. "There's been an accident. I've just come from the airport. It's her granddaughter. They don't know if she's going to live."

"The congregation will pray for her," the reverend says. "Is there an address where the congregation can send their condolences?"

"It's in the jungle," Seymour says. "There are snakes."

When Seymour arrives back at the house, Herbie is incinerating Theo's possessions in a bonfire. Angelina is on her cell. "The employment agency," she says, palming the mouthpiece. "I'm working on a replacement."

Kenji's dirge wafts through the trees and across the lake. Smoke from the blaze coils around the sagging cedar boughs.

"I was cleaning out Theo's room," Angelina says. "I found this."

The Rail Spur Record
Harry Shapka, Senior Reporter.

"Even I've got one of those," Seymour says. He tosses the card into the flames. "The guy's a drunk."

"Maybe so," Angelina says, "but I punched the redial button on Theo's phone. Her last call was to the newspaper."

"In that case," Seymour says, "we've got *two* problems."

The Dollar Store's first customer of the day was crouched in the doorway when George Elliott arrived. "Hope you haven't been waiting long. Town bylaw says we can't open before seven."

The stranger followed George inside, handed him a photo.

"Know her?"

The picture showed a bulging bicep roped around the neck of a young woman.

"I've seen that picture before," George said. "That's Angelina DuBois, my sales clerk. She quit last year."

"Angelina DuBois, huh?" The stranger ignited a cigarette.

George said, "Can't have you doing that in here, sir."

The stranger walked to the door and flicked the cigarette into the street. "Know where I can find her?"

"Seymour Barnes used to date her," he said, "but they broke up, and Angelina left town. He works up at the Shackleford place."

"How long if I walk it?"

160

"If you leave now", he glanced at his wristwatch, then pointed the way, "you might make it by nightfall." He considered mentioning that the jackals roamed freely after dark, but decided against it.

The stranger grabbed a lighter from the counter and tested its flame.

"Those are two for a dollar," George said.

The stranger selected a second, offering in place of a dollar a look that caused a chill to race up George Elliott's spine.

V

The phone rang.

"Harry? Arlene."

They'd met twice since Barry's funeral. If what the therapist believed was true — that the girl passing herself off as the former fashion model was an imposter, and that Suzanne Shackleford was likely dead — then Harry was sitting on the story of his career. By comparison, the magazine profile of the heiress was filler.

"Don't hang up," Arlene said. She was hyperventilating. "I'm going through the recordings now."

While waiting, Harry imagined himself the author of a bestseller: *Crack investigative journalist Harry Shapka turns his hand to fiction . . . Ladies and gentlemen, please welcome* —

"Found them," Arlene said. "All my sessions with Suzanne. We met about a dozen times. Of course I can't turn the recordings over to Norval. You know, therapist-patient privilege. But I can let him hear a snippet, right?"

Therapist-patient privilege. The phrase spun like an upended bicycle wheel inside Harry's whiskey-soaked brain.

"How," he asked her, "can there be such a privilege if the patient is missing and presumed dead?"

"Good point, Harry," Arlene said. "But wouldn't her death have to be established before I release the recordings?"

"Why don't I come over?"

Other offices on the pier were already closed. Tobacco smoke and a dreamy Latin beat streamed through the open doors of Café Casa. Yachtsmen chatted nearby; a young couple snuggled. Otherwise it was just him and Arlene and two highballs in Sailors, a new waterfront bar.

"I have her medical file, Harry," she said. "Have a look. It has copies of Suzanne's X-ray reports. The recordings and the file would be all the evidence any court would need."

They agreed to meet at the police station in the morning.

Back home, Harry desperately wanted to call someone and boast of his good fortune, but there was no one. So he poured himself another drink and returned to his resignation letter.

Harry heard glass shatter out back. The cat he assumed. Those empty Scotch bottles on the porch. He switched on the porch light and unbolted the door. "Meow!" he said. Shards of glass were sprinkled on the landing. He could see the cat's luminous green eyes watching from the high grass.

Fireworks were packaged in the building across the alley. It was occupied for only a few months of the year. When vacant, as it was now, the lot was a popular haunt for lovers and dope smokers. He noticed a pickup truck near the loading ramp. A pair of cigarettes glowed from within.

Harry staggered back inside and ransacked the closet for the broom and dustpan. He slipped on his Toronto Blue Jays ball cap and swept the porch, depositing the glass into a plastic supermarket bag. At the trash can in the alley he stopped to consider his dilapidated rental. It occurred to him for the first time that this woebegone dump was an apt metaphor for his woebegone life.

"Hey, Harry . . . "

Two sets of headlights on the highway inched closer together as the road dipped to within a few metres of the lake.

When the SUV slowed, the pickup swerved in behind, its engine idling unevenly. This was far from town, on a remote stretch of road.

Their bumpers met. The driver of the SUV pumped the brakes. When they skidded to a stop a figure slipped from the pickup. A horn sounded, and the pickup sped off. Someone climbed out of the SUV.

"I saw the flames from my bedroom window," said George. "My Dollar Store."

"Looks like vandals," said Norval.

"I suppose."

"Somebody out there don't like you, George?"

"I can't imagine why."

The back door of the reporter's bungalow had been left open. A printout of the resignation letter was stuck to the fridge door with a wad of gum.

"Dear Fuckface," it began. "High noon, you and me, in the octagon."

When someone disappears mysteriously, police routinely check bank records. This wasn't the case with Harry. First, no one considered his sudden absence mysterious; he had talked recently of little else. And Rail Spur Savings & Loan didn't have an account in his name. Harry had invested all his earnings at the Last Call Bar & Grill.

Hundreds of people attended Arlene's funeral. The *Record* published a recent photo, the new and improved incarnation, under the headline, "Slippery Roads Suspected in Fatal Crash." She was remembered by friends and associates as a caring professional and a devoted wife and mother. At the graveside service Simon & Garfunkel's "Bridge Over Troubled Water" was piped over loudspeakers mounted in the trees.

Angelina heard a *thump-thump* just as the Jag was rounding a bend in the road. She pulled over and examined the undercarriage, but all she found was a clump of fur snagged in the wheel well — or was that hair? She backed the car up, stopping alongside the carcass — or is that a body?

The man was gripping his left foot and groaning. He had a long mane of tangled hair on one side of his head and a bloody, hairless mess on the other.

She lowered the driver's window.

"Funny place for a nap," she said. "Middle of the highway is for white lines and roadkill. Which are you?"

"Very funny, lady. How about a lift to the hospital?"

Angelina helped the man into the back seat. He smelled homeless.

"You're lucky it's only your toes," she said. "If you had been lying the other way, it would have been your coconut."

"I don't feel lucky."

"You trying to off yourself, mister? Is that it?"

She reached into her purse and counted out a few OxyContin.

"These should take the edge off," she said.

Then, because she was an unlicensed and uninsured motorist, she dangled a few hundred dollars in his face.

"Let's keep this to ourselves, okay?"

The man lunged at the money.

"I'll have to see what my lawyer says."

"Bet you have a whole team on retainer, huh?"

Angelina got a better look at the man while he was being fitted for a cast and having his head bandaged. He had a shaggy beard, but he looked familiar. Afterwards they stopped at a drive-in burger joint.

"Are you from around here?" she asked.

The dope made him chatty. "I have a cabin up on the ridge."

"Sure you do. What's your name?"

"My friends call me Phil."

"What do the rest of us call you?"

"Phil."

And then it came to her.

"Phil 'Success International' Frank. I don't fuckin' believe it!"

"So you've heard my CDs. That was in another life, I'm afraid."

"What happened to the girlfriend? A bit of a pie wagon?"

"Iris. That whore cleaned me out. A second burger, maybe?"

Angelina honked at the waitress.

"The self-help gig has run its course; everybody's doing it these days, stealing from each other. I've been at the library every day, looking for work online."

"What kind?"

"I used to be a lawyer."

"I'm guessing that didn't end well either."

"I got into some trouble. My licence got yanked. Then they found out about my law degree."

"Online or mail order?"

"Homemade, actually. Fooled plenty of people, though."

Angelina gave him the rest of her Oxy and left him hobbling up a trail leading to Ridgeway Cabins, which a sign said were CLOSED FOR THE SEASON.

She was sitting on a bench in the bus station, a figure so slight it appeared that in a strong wind she could snap like a cracker. The youngster, asleep, was wedged into her side.

Seymour read from a slip of paper, "Are you Con-stan-tina?"

She reminded him of a fawn that sometimes drank from the creek behind his cabin: poised for flight. The extent of her communication seemed to be no, yes, and a frightened smile. Their possessions fit into a single suitcase.

Constantina's daughter could speak enough English to be understood. Her name, she announced, was Paulina. It sounded like a boast.

"And I'm ten and a half."

On the drive back to the house the girl told Seymour about their Yucatan village and the father who had died.

"We Maya," she explained. "Mexico Indian."

Seymour moved into a spare room and let the newcomers have the guest house. Constantina went to work immediately; he rarely saw her at rest. If she wasn't doing laundry, she was cooking or folding clothes or waxing floors. He tried explaining she needn't work on Sundays.

"*Si, si,*" she said, and continued labouring.

Paulina acted like she'd been let loose in an amusement park. She constructed sandcastles on the beach and tried snaring birds with a simple trap. She was never successful, but never grew discouraged. Seymour was aware of her watching him dive off the end of the dock. When he surfaced she was in the water, but the girl couldn't swim and had to be retrieved like a beer can from the bottom of the lake.

The youngster shinnied up every worthy tree on the property and fell from a slippery elm. When the doctor was fitting her for a sling, she didn't leak a tear. Seymour drove the pair into town on shopping days and filled out the application for the little one to attend school. When the arm mended Seymour and the girl began racing around the yard on bicycles.

He and Paulina developed a language, part sign, part words.

"Who tree house boy?" Paulina wanted to know. She stretched her eyes into slits, mimed someone blowing a horn. Seymour hadn't seen Kenji in months. He assumed he'd returned to Japan or been turned over to one of Barry's pals, a bequest.

For Herbie, Paulina filled her cheeks with air and scowled.

"Looks bad," she said. "Smells good."

Suzanne — Miss Mean — was easy: a downturned face.

As for Seymour himself, Paulina was able to get across that she had never met a man who tied his hair in a ponytail and wore red sneakers.

168

The more Seymour saw of Constantina, the more he was intrigued. She appeared to exist on a planet of her own creation. There were no leisure activities in her world. It was work, eat, sleep, and dote on the girl.

VI

Phil is making his way up the trail. The cast is off, but he's limping. He's lugging a bag of groceries, many of them shoplifted. Descending the trail is the only other squatter at Ridgeway Cabins.

"You in cabin five?" Phil asks. "I see you doing chin-ups every morning."

"What's it to ya?"

"Just being neighbourly is all." Phil slides a boxed pie from his shopping bag. "Peach. Drop by if you fancy a wedge. I'm in three. That's the one — "

"I can count, dipshit."

"You've got quite the potty mouth," Phil says. "Looks like you've had your nose broken. Wonder why."

"A country and western bar." she says. "Fuckin' cowboys ganged up on me."

Phil leads his guest to cabin three and hands over a couple of Oxys.

"Got a question for you," he says. "Used to be a couple of bulldykes near where I lived. Both of 'em had short hair and dressed like men. If they're both into women, why dress like men?"

"I'm looking for someone," she says, sliding a photo across the table. "Seen her?"

"I haven't," Phil says. "Nope."

"There's a reward."

"I'll keep my eyes peeled."

The final step in the plan had stalled. The problem was money — there was too much of it. In addition to the bank accounts, which were easily closed by Angelina, the Shacklefords had amassed more wealth than Seymour had imagined. There were bonds, stocks, shares, land. Neither of them knew how to convert such things into cash. The only person they knew who did was Cornell. Asking the family lawyer to assist would sound an alarm.

"Leave it with me," Angelina told Seymour. "I know just the man for the job."

"Yeah? Who?"

"A white-collar Herbie."

At first Seymour was pissed off. He recalled her objection to Herbie's participation: the more who knew, the greater the risk, right? But his mind was on Constantina and Paulina. He was happy to let Angelina take care of the paperwork.

All that really mattered to Seymour was that he now possessed more money than he could ever spend. He felt he knew what Angelina would do with her share: clothes, travel, dope. Her experience with cosmetic surgery had also convinced her she needed more. She often talked about getting a boob job.

Seymour was less sure of where to go and what to do when the dust settled. He hadn't travelled much. He preferred T-shirts to neckties — which he had tired of — and barbecues on the beach to restaurants requiring a knowledge of French or Italian.

Phil Frank's CDs had helped, sort of. But they were of little use now that his pockets were full. He paddled out to Wigwam Rock one afternoon and dumped the entire set overboard.

Adios, Phil.

And the money? Seymour was thankful that he'd never again have to fret about having any. He remembered what Suzanne had said: *What does one do with everything?* And although he wasn't averse to vacations, the place he wanted to live out his days was on Tullaine Lake, or at least another spot like it. Nothing gave him greater joy than sitting in his canoe, watching the sun make its torpid way across the heavens, a nibble at the end of his fishing line.

Such thoughts were invariably replaced by reminders of his transgressions. He hadn't enjoyed a single night of uninterrupted sleep since that day in the woods with the real Suzanne. He missed his cabin, slept in the big house with the window wide open. With every howl from a jackal, at every crack of a branch, he was up and out of bed, sleep impossible.

The others he'd wronged populated Seymour's dreams. Theodora, Barry, the reporter, Arlene — they wouldn't let go. When he thought of Suzanne and Theo, of the kindness shown him, he understood he'd eliminated those he should have spared and allied himself with those most deserving of a killing. His life, he realized, *had* become a stupid movie script.

"Have you seen the gun?" Angelina asks.

Seymour is sitting on the beach; Paulina is practising the crawl.

"Who you gonna shoot?"

"Jackals, maybe," she says. "They've been seen up on the ridge. Don't worry, I'll give it back."

He tosses her the backpack.

"Careful," he says. "It's loaded."

Angelina was trying to score some meth in Cobalt when Mr. President passed her on the street. The former jailhouse tyrant was wearing a disguise that would fool any cop: a dress, heels, lipstick, the works. She was wearing the same outfit, sitting on a park bench, when Angelina was driving through Rail Spur a few weeks later. Crazy bitch was getting closer.

She finds Phil at the periodical rack in the library.

"Looking for work?"

"My foot still hurts. The doctor says I'm going to be a gimp."

She passes him a vial of Oxy. He swallows a few and stuffs the vial in his pocket.

"I might have a job for you," she says. "Is there anything you *won't* do?"

"I was a motivational speaker," he replies. "Does that answer your question?"

Al Watson was weighing an important decision when his desk phone began flashing: should he lunch on the carrot sticks Merna had packed or feast on jumbo dogs with fellow officers? His deliberations became doubly agonizing when he remembered it was two-for-one Tuesday at the Beefmobile.

There was a rap at the door.

"Long distance, Sarge. From Vancouver. The caller says it's important."

"I'm a cosmetic surgeon," Dr. Beaverstock said. "Confidentiality is vital to our business. Without it, we'd be finished."

The surgeon explained that he'd performed a series of procedures on a patient residing in Rail Spur. Her name was Suzanne Shackleford.

"I know the family," Al said.

Dr. Beaverstock explained that blood was routinely drawn from patients prior to a procedure; a backup supply was required in the event of an emergency.

"It's a formality," he said. "I've never had to use any."

"Uh-huh . . . "

A temp had misunderstood instructions and had inadvertently forwarded Suzanne's blood type to a national DNA data resource centre. Its computer was programmed to supply the donor's identity.

"Computers confuse me, doctor. Can we switch to English?"

"It would appear that the woman identifying herself as Miss Shackleford appears not to be that person, officer. We were alerted that the blood we have in storage belongs to someone called Patti Markham. Correction facilities take a blood sample from all inmates. Each is banked at the resource centre, thus the match."

"Are you trying to tell me," Al asked the doctor, "that we now have this information as a result of someone in your office . . . fucking up?"

"A temp," Beaverstock reminded.

"Doctor?"

"Sergeant Watson?"

"Excellent police work."

Al popped a carrot stick into his mouth and called Norval.

Phil pounds on the door of cabin five.

"Daylight in the swamps, Mr President!"

"Ever heard of phoning first?" she hollers.

"Neither of us has a phone," Phil says.

"Whattya want?"

"I've got some Oxy."

"Why didn't you say so?" She opens the door. "Coffee?"

"No time," Phil says. "The girl you're looking for is on the road below the cabins."

Mr. President pushes him aside and charges down the trail. Phil catches up to her on the railway tracks.

"Best stop right there," he says. About ten metres of rusty track separates them. He's pointing the Smith & Wesson.

Phil fires two shots, both off the mark.

Mr. President flashes him the finger.

Phil fires three more times; each bullet, like the previous two, lands in a distant jurisdiction.

174

"I'm gonna crush your balls, man!"

Phil closes his eyes and squeezes off the final round.

Bull's eye.

Just about the last person Seymour expected to see sauntering around the side of the house that morning was the police chief.

"Howdy, Barnes!" Norval boomed at Seymour. "Boss around?"

Angelina came out on the veranda.

"Is something wrong, chief? Constantina! Bring Norval some iced tea? The poor man's dying out here!"

The policeman slapped a folder on the patio table.

"Seen the For Sale sign out on the highway, Suzanne," he said. "There's been a Shackleford in town as long as I can remember."

Constantina arrived with his drink.

"Reason I dropped by, a motorist pulled over outside of town to answer the call of nature. He found these."

Suzanne's medical files. Herbie was supposed to have burned them.

"That Jamieson woman's signature is on every page," Norval said. "Any idea how your private records ended up out there?"

"You're the policeman."

"Arlene's vehicle was found a long way from where our urinator found them. It doesn't make a whole lot of sense, does it? The way they were scattered, it looks like they'd been tossed from a moving vehicle."

She scanned the files. If someone cared to cross-reference the information, they were done.

"What do you think we should do?" he asked.

She slid the folder across the table. "I have no need of them."

The chief sipped his tea.

"You'll have to sign a release form," he said.

He handed her a pen; she attached Suzanne's signature.

"Too bad about Theo," he said. "New girl working out all right?"

Kenji was playing his flute at the side of the house. The chief asked, "That the Chinaman I keep hearing about?"

"He's Japanese."

"Same difference, ain't it?"

Before driving off, he said, "That little girl, she'll have to put some clothes on when she comes into town."

In the beginning Angelina had been an unwilling participant in Seymour's plot. Now, his interest waning, he was happy to let her become its chief architect. While she wrestled with business matters, working with her guy up at Ridgeway Cabins, he was invariably off somewhere with Constantina and Paulina.

On the housekeeper's days off they paddled out to the islands; evenings they drove into town for ice cream or swam until dark. He and the girl built a raft with lumber left over from the resort project.

He bought them clothes, a flat screen TV. He tricked Paulina into getting the address of their bank in Mexico.

From Cobalt he wired hundreds of thousands of dollars into the account. He was afraid that if he were to tell Constantina, she and the girl would leave. Everyone else in his life had.

He was also concerned about Angelina and Herbie. They were increasingly uncivil with Constantina.

"It's like," Angelina remarked one day, Paulina on the swing, "they've just climbed down from the vines. It's like they're still evolving."

"Harm either of them," he hissed, "and you'll be next."

The longer it took for the transactions to be finalized, the more miserable Angelina became. But if they wanted all Shackleford proceeds, they had to be patient. Papers had to be signed. There were protocols, procedures. Phil was no lawyer; Angelina, who'd had a few, could see that, but he knew a lot more than her and Seymour.

"What's with all the red tape?" Angelina asked Phil one day. They'd been working on a land transaction all morning. "Every form asks the same questions: name, address, telephone number. Only difference is, one form is printed on blue paper, the other one is on yellow. Why can't all the questions be on one form?"

"If everything was that simple," Phil said, "this wouldn't be Canada."

One afternoon Seymour found himself pondering Oprah's test for love: the palpitating heart, the wobbly knees. While out walking with Constantina he felt certain. That night, the child asleep, he approached the guest house. The door squeaked open. Seymour consulted his phrasebook.

"*Buenas noches, señorita.*"

Seymour saw Angelina with her white-collar Herbie entering The Last Call. Later in the week he was parked at a produce stand east of town, Constantina picking out some corn. A BMW sped by. He couldn't make out the driver, but the passenger's window was rolled down. Angelina was inside, laughing. Something was up: Angelina didn't laugh.

Though the partnership had been successful, their suspicion of each other was mounting. Each was guardian of the other's charade. Distrust had settled between them like a toxin.

He'd sensed for some time that she was plotting against him. Her soul seemed to roil with invisible fault lines. He noticed her wearing a bracelet identical to the one Suzanne had worn that day in the forest. Identical to the bracelet on the wall of Herbie's trailer. They'd sacrificed it to the waters below Wigwam Rock, hadn't they?

Early the following day Seymour drove to the Chevron and requested a brake job for the pickup. The courtesy car was a Mazda. Angelina usually went out for her morning drive before he was up, so the next day he woke early and drove out to a service road, waiting for her to pass. When she did, he tried following, but couldn't keep the Jag in sight, so he turned around. Moments later another vehicle whizzed by. It was a BMW. Seymour made another U-turn.

Up the highway the Jag and the BMW were parked together. Seymour ditched the Mazda and tracked the pair to a clearing in the woods. Their conversation was animated. The man's hair was blond and long. It was tied in a ponytail.

After they'd left, he searched the clearing. He picked up his truck and continued on to his cabin. He passed most of the day composing a letter. It explained everything. Back at the house he found Paulina reciting nursery rhymes.

"*Vámonos!*" he said.

She leaped like a pup at the heavy steel box tucked under his arm. They climbed the rope ladder to the tree house.

"*Qué?*" she asked, tapping the box.

He made her repeat everything in English: if he had to go away, she was to retrieve the box. There was a great secret inside — and the card of a lawyer who spoke some Spanish. They were not to tell anyone else. Seymour leaned out the window of the tree house and slid the box to the centre of the roof. He handed Paulina the spare key.

"*Comprende?*"

"*Sí,*" she giggled. "*Entiendo.*"

Seymour couldn't get the stranger out of his head. The meeting in the clearing, the bracelet, The Last Call, the ponytail — what did it all mean? Nothing good. He woke that night in a sweat, Constantina breathing softly at his side.

They push off from shore. Herbie reclines in the stern, untangling his fishing line; Seymour faces land, working the oars. A weeping Paulina waves from shore; she'd wanted to join them. He can see the school bus waiting on the highway, Constantina chasing the girl with a switch.

They round the point; Seymour hauls in the oars. They drift.

"I think you got a problem," Herbie says.

The wind picks up, whitecaps slap the hull. Seymour rows to the nearest island. There's a lean-to on the beach where the local teens party. Seymour builds a fire; Herbie rolls some BC bud.

"I followed them for a couple of days, just like you asked me to," Herbie says. "Yesterday they went into Gray's."

Stan Gray owned Rail Spur's Gun & Reel Shop.

"They bought a gun and some ammo," Herbie says.

The wind dies down, clouds pass. Tullaine Lake sparkles invitingly. Herbie flicks the roach into the fire.

By sundown trees yield to the wind. The sky darkens. Paulina finds him in the gazebo.

"Come," she implores, seizing Seymour's hand. "Mama say eat."

The girl flinches at the first crack of thunder.

"Soon," he says, shooing her away.

Seymour can see Angelina's silhouette in the bedroom window. He crosses the yard and climbs the stairs, the Smith & Wesson clenched in his hand. A sliver of light escapes from under her door.

"Enter," she says.

There is a beguiling twist to her Botox-swollen lips. A sweet smell hangs in the humid night air.

The sky splits like a *piñata* just as Constantina steps naked from the lake. She walks into the garden and looks up at the house. Warm rain sluices between her tiny charcoal breasts.

At dawn Constantina heard footsteps on the porch. An envelope was pushed under the door. She was preparing breakfast when Paulina finished translating the letter and closed her dictionary. It said they were to be packed and on the highway by noon. The severance pay, a bundle of cash, was generous.

But where was Seymour?

They were waiting for the taxi when Paulina ignored her mother's remonstrations and scaled the wall, scampering up the rope ladder. In the tree house she balanced on the window ledge, but she couldn't reach the box.

Kenji dropped down from a branch onto the roof. He carried the box to the taxi.

"*Gracias,*" Constantina said. "Goodbye, Kenji."

They caught the midnight bus to the coast. It sped through the mountains and into the valley. As the girl slept, Constantina examined the contents of the box — all that money, a lawyer's card, the photo of a beautiful woman.

Constantina placed a hand over her womb. She hoped the baby would have his smile.

He opens his eyes to a black sky dusted with stars. He knows neither where he is nor who. It's cold, and he can't feel his limbs.

And then it's morning. He has been moved, but by whom? He sees Suzanne's mauve kerchief stretched out across the sand. Theo's hair ribbon is snagged on a branch. A Toronto Blue Jays cap skims like a toy sailboat along a shallow stream.

He is not alone. He's unable to determine by which of the senses he knows this to be true, but he does. He begins to slip away.

When he regains consciousness a jackal is licking blood from his face. Others wrestle meat from bone. He hears the beasts yipping and howling, skirmishing amongst themselves. The victor saunters by, a foot clamped between its teeth. Seymour recognizes his red sneaker.

Norval was saying, "We got ourselves a little mystery, folks."

Before him on the table was a spread of photos. To one side was the glossy of Suzanne left behind by Harry. Alongside it were more recent shots taken by Sandi.

"Damned if I can tell the difference," said the police chief.

"These are two different people," Sandi said.

Norval opened a second folder. It contained a copy of Suzanne's medical records, Patti Markham's Wanted poster, and the snapshot Al had retrieved from the fugitive's cell.

"Do we have anything else?" Norval asked.

"There's the blood work," Al said. "It doesn't match."

Sandi said, "The X-rays won't either."

There was a knock at the door. A constable handed over a manila envelope. It contained the results of the fingerprints Norval secured on his recent visit to the Shackleford's. The report confirmed their suspicions.

"Al," he said, "would you give the young lady and me a moment?"

For her assistance in the case Sandi would be given exclusive access to all case files and background info. Quotations published in *Glitter* could be colourful and candid, but, when requested, from unnamed sources. In return Sandi would portray officers Spikes and the aptly named Watson as the greatest investigative geniuses since Sherlock Holmes.

The reporter left; Al returned. The agreement the two policemen worked out included sharing the spotlight and mutually complimentary commentary. The sergeant was assured a long reign in Rail Spur; Norval would conclude his career with a high-profile launch to the town's only home security business.

The constable poked his head into the office.

"The boys are ready, chief," he said. He was wearing a bulletproof vest.

The Toyota turns off the highway and rattles to a stop in the driveway. A pool party is in progress.

"Pizza!" announces Archie Meeks. He's wearing a paper hat. "Five large with anchovies, three mediums with cheese and mushrooms . . . "

Archie has been fired from the *Record*, Ed Leatherdale told him, for being "a lazy, duplicitous bastard." He is thinking about going back to school.

Suzanne's newly embellished breasts are bursting out of a halter top. Sliding along her wrist is the bracelet that began as a fashion model's inexpensive accessory, was sacrificed to an aboriginal spirit and had resided for a time in the cabin of a mutant.

Granny has been retrieved from the care home and left to wilt in the heat. Her chin glistens with spittle.

"Hey, sonny," she says to Archie, the first words to pass her lips in years. "Be a sport, pass me a slice, then wheel me into the shade. I don't want to miss this."

A phalanx of deputies fans out through the woods, badges glinting where the sun penetrates the canopy. Another contingent of policemen arrives by boat. Kenji sits in the cherry tree playing a livelier version of his only melody, the Dodger jacket draped across his shoulders. Fabiana, the new Guatemalan housekeeper, distributes refreshments. Her son Ramon splashes in the shallow end of the pool. Herbie lifeguards.

Seymour mans the barbecue. We know it's him because of the red sneakers, that ponytail snapping like the tail of a frisky canine. When the copter swoops low, he removes his sunglasses and squints into the sun. For just a moment we see that around the eyes the Shackleford handyman resembles — no, no, it can't be.

Photo by Alex Waterhouse-Hayward

Don McLellan has worked as a journalist in Canada, South Korea and Hong Kong. His debut collection of short stories, In the Quiet After Slaughter (Libros Libertad), was a 2009 ReLit Award finalist. He currently edits a trade magazine in Vancouver.